DEVIL'S GUARD
THE REAL STORY

DEVIL'S GUARD
THE REAL STORY

ERIC MEYER

First published in the United Kingdom in 2010 by Swordworks Books

ISBN 978-1906512453

Typeset by Swordworks Books
Printed and bound in the UK & US
A catalogue record of this book is available
from the British Library

Cover design by Swordworks Books
www.swordworks.co.uk

Dedicated to those who have fallen on
all sides in both Indochina wars

FOREWORD

There have been various 'true' stories written about the so-called 'Devil's Guard', a contingent of exclusively former Waffen-SS soldiers fighting against the Viet Minh in Vietnam, or Indochina as it was known in the early 1950's. My research suggested that there was never such a unit. Instead, all Foreign Legion units were comprised of men from many different backgrounds, although some inevitably had more than their fair share of former German soldiers, many of them Waffen-SS.

Many supposed 'true' accounts of former Waffen-SS involvement in French Indochina seem singularly lacking in the verifiable detail that is the essence of a reasonable historical account. I interviewed a number of former soldiers who fought in that war, and it was from one of these Legionnaires that I obtained this story. Is it 'true', the reader may ask? The answer is sadly yes and no. Yes, it is based on what I learned from people who were actually there. Yes, the details, dates, places, units and equipment could all be verified. But did these particular events ever happen as recorded in this story? That is like answering the question 'who Shot JFK' on that fateful day in Dallas, Texas. We shall never know. Certainly I believe it is based on a true story, but beyond that sadly vague definition it is impossible to fully verify. But it could have happened....

I hope and trust you enjoy reading it as much as I enjoyed writing it.

Eric Meyer

INTRODUCTION

Following the German defeat in 1945, Waffen-SS, Heinrich Himmler's private army, were largely hunted down by the victorious Allies and many were imprisoned. Post-war recruitment by the French Foreign Legion amongst former German soldiers netted a substantial number of former Waffen-SS troopers. After all, they were being hunted by the victorious allies and the French offered them a new identity, in return for them using their renowned fighting skills for their new employers. Until 1947, there was little control on who joined the Legion and recruit backgrounds were not extensively checked. After 1947 things tightened up, although without doubt many former SS continued to join up.

Many of these soldiers were sent to Indochina, newly restored to France following the defeat of the Japanese. Indochina, of course, is now known as Vietnam. The French returned to Indochina determined to rule as a colonial overlord, trampling over a variety of agreements made with the native population, represented by the regime of Ho Chi Minh. The result was a series of battles in which the French became increasingly embattled and called upon more and more troops to reinforce what to many was already a lost cause. Perhaps the Americans would have done well to read the history books before they embarked on their disastrous Vietnamese debacle.

Nonetheless, there is no doubt that troops on all sides fought courageously, notably the French Foreign Legion, the Paratroops and the Colonial Infantry who bore much of the brunt of the fighting. Ranged against them were the forces of the Viet Minh, a forerunner to the Viet Cong. Led by the notable military leader Vo Nguyen Giap. Giap was a thorn in the side of the French and his clever leadership and organization led eventually to the French defeat at Dien Bien Phu, which marked the end of French ambitions in the region.

This book documents an account of a mission to attack Giap personally. It is based upon personal accounts and much of it is undocumented. However, there can be little doubt that French military minds would have wrestled with the problem of how to rid themselves of this turbulent leader.

CHAPTER ONE

Avril rapidly emptied his MAT49 submachine gun into the oncoming horde of Viet Minh, heard the firing pin click on an empty clip, reloaded and desperately opened fire again, seeing his bullets smack home into the Vietnamese fanatics hurling themselves bodily at his French troops. The firefight, one kilometre west of the town of Mao Khe, had begun as a simple skirmish. The lieutenant's company, part of the 6th Colonial Parachute Battalion led by Captain Charles Balmain, attached to Mobile Group 2, had been marching into Mao Khe when they ran headlong into General Giap's 320th Division, who were themselves rushing to support the massed Viet Minh attack on the town.

Vo Nguyen Giap was born on August 25th, 1911, and had risen to become leader of the Vietnam People's Army, he was both a politician and a formidable soldier. He was also a journalist and served as a politburo member of the Lao Dong Party. Giap was the most prominent military commander, besides Ho

Chi Minh, during the Indochina war and was responsible for all major operations and leadership throughout the war. Clever, cunning, calculating, he was a man who didn't like to lose and would sacrifice his own troops and civilians in huge numbers if he thought that it was necessary to win the war. The swift mobilisation of several divisions of troops to surround Mao Khe bore all the hallmarks of his effective brand of military strategy.

Initially, two reconnaissance platoons had exchanged fire, both commanders rushed up more and more men. It was a bloodbath. Even though they were killing the Viet Minh like pigs in a slaughterhouse, they were outnumbered by a vastly superior force.

Avril heard screams and shouts from his men as they were hit by enemy rounds, the wet 'thud' as the bullets smashed through tissue and bone to destroy his command, soldier by soldier. Captain Balmain was one of the early casualties, struck by a bullet fired from an SKS rifle, the fraternal gift of the Soviet Union who was desperate to win favour with the Vietnamese communists. He was dead, his body lying on the ground with the back of his head missing where the bullet had drilled through his skull.

The French frequently faced the SKS, a Soviet semi-automatic carbine chambered for the 7.62 round, designed in 1945 by Sergei Simonov. The SKS had a conventional carbine layout, with a wooden stock and no pistol grip. Most versions were fitted with an integral folding bayonet which hinged down from the end of the barrel, and some versions were even equipped with a grenade launching attachment. Another product of

Russian and Chinese generosity, the SKS was cheap, easy to strip and maintain in jungle conditions, and an effective killer in the short range exchanges of gunfire that were so common in the jungle.

"Retreat, fall back men, we need to form a tighter perimeter," Avril shouted.

His paras, veterans of the war in Indochina, slowly edged back, firing desperately to give themselves time to form a stronger defence. Avril sighted a small hill, more of a hillock, about a hundred metres behind them.

"Run, men, run, we need to get on that hill, follow me!"

They ran, a stumbling, scrambling desperate flight. Some fell, hit by Viet Minh fire.

"Don't stop for the wounded, there's no time, just run!" Avril shouted, urging them on.

He turned to fire a burst into the oncoming Vietnamese, seeing two of them fall. Then he turned, legs pumping as he ran up the hill, urging his men, "Run, we're nearly there, run!"

A bullet tore into the sleeve of his shirt, a near miss, he felt another clip his right boot, then flatten itself into a nearby rock. But he was there leaping over the rocks that lay scattered at the top of the hill, flung himself flat on the ground, his men jumping down nearby beginning to fire on the pursuing enemy. He switched magazines and began firing short bursts into the Viet Minh who were hurtling towards them. Three more paras went down, the rest were sheltering behind the rocks, pouring an increasing amount of fire at the Viet Minh. The Vietnamese guerrillas began to falter, seeing their comrades falling all around them. Then they turned and ran back, seeing still more of their numbers fall as they took cover behind the trees and rocks surrounding the hill.

Avril drew breath and shouted at his men to cease fire. The occasional shot came up at them from the Viet Minh, but none were well aimed.

"Save your ammunition, men," he called, "they'll be back soon and we'll need every bullet. Sergeant Hassiba," his second in command, now that Balmain was dead.

"We need a count of the ammunition, find out what we have left. It'll be a long time before headquarters knows we're stuck here, until then we need to make the supplies last."

Sergeant Karim Hassiba was an Algerian and a veteran of the colonial infantry who'd seen service in the Second World War as a green private soldier, fighting with the Free French forces through Nazi Germany. He doubled away to check the remaining ordnance. Avril then gave orders to another Algerian, Corporal Wahid Farouk, to tally their remaining food and water. They could be there for a long stay.

The men slumped down, lighting cigarettes and taking hasty gulps of water from their water bottles. He hoped it was only water, but it was hardly the time to check. He got out his binoculars and scanned the wooded ground around the bottom of the hill. The Viet Minh were there, hiding but occasionally moving from cover to cover. They were all around. Breaking out from this hill was going to be hard and bloody.

"Private Laroche. Get on the radio and contact headquarters, let me know when you get through." He stood and watched the radioman begin warming up the radio, then went to do the rounds of his position. It was grim. A total of sixty seven men left from the original one hundred and thirty that set out on this mission, nearly half were dead or missing. Ammunition was less than forty rounds per man, a total of eleven hand grenades, food and water for twenty four hours at most. He went back to the radioman.

"Laroche, have you got through yet?"

"Sir, the radio is broken, completely broken."

He showed Avril a hole torn out of the metal in the case where an enemy bullet had gone through the equipment, wrecking it beyond repair.

"See what you can do Laroche, keep trying to fix it."

"Yes, Sir," the radioman looked doubtful, "I'll do what I can."

Avril called Sergeant Hassiba to discuss their options. He valued the tough Algerian's opinion, gathered in more than a dozen tight spots. Algerians and Moroccans formed the backbone of the French colonial units, many of them made exceptional soldiers, brave and resourceful. Good to have in a situation like this.

"Sergeant, I think reinforcements could take more time than we have left to us."

"Yes, I think so too. We need to get out of this trap, Sir, before we're completely out of food and ammunition."

"Any ideas?"

"Whichever way we go, we'll have to fight through the Viets. Wait until night then break through."

Avril checked his watch. It was almost two thirty in the afternoon.

"Not enough ammunition to hold them off and wait that

long Sergeant. We need to go soon, before they attack and run us out of ammunition."

"Then, we…" Hassiba stopped.

They could see the Viets had begun massing at the bottom of the hill. They didn't seem unduly concerned that the French might open fire. Clearly their commander was no fool, he knew the French troops would be dangerously low on ammunition.

"You'd better get the men ready Sergeant, they'll be attacking soon."

"And then?" Hassiba asked. "If we fight off this attack? What then?"

"We'll fight them, Sergeant, and as soon as possible we'll try to break out."

"Fight them with what, Sir?"

Avril sighed, the Algerian was right, their ammunition was almost exhausted. After that, there would be nothing left but surrender. The prospect of showing the white flag to these ugly Asian monkeys was not pleasant. The Viets were known for their brutality to captured French troops, often using them for bayonet practice and gruesome games of torture and execution.

"Tell the men single shots only. No automatic fire, they need to make every shot count. As soon as we beat them back, we'll try and get out. Make sure the men are ready to move the second I give the order."

"Yes, Sir." Hassiba saluted then ran off to pass the orders to the men.

They waited, some chain smoking, the Catholics amongst

them fingering rosary beads, the Muslims reading small, worn looking copies of the Koran. Avril watched the Viets milling around, the officers and commissars shouting orders, getting the men into position, firing them up with stirring party rhetoric.

One man stood out from the rag-taggle band of guerrillas, giving orders to the men. He was dressed in what appeared to be a soiled cream linen safari suit, an incongruity in the jungle war. He wore an old fedora hat with a red bandana wrapped around its brim. He carried no pack, just a pistol in one hand. Next to him a soldier carried a loudhailer. The man in the suit gave an order and the soldier passed him a microphone attached to the loudhailer. There were a series of clicks and buzzes. Then his voice came clearly up to them in fluent French.

"Men! Soldiers who are fighting for the French colonialists. This is not your war! France has enslaved your own countries, Morocco, Algeria, here in Vietnam too. They are keeping you in chains to exploit you. My name is Commissar Colonel Min. I speak for the People's Revolutionary Army, the Viet Minh."

The Viet Minh, the League for the Independence of Vietnam, was a national independence movement founded in South China on May 19th, 1941. The Viet Minh initially formed to seek independence for Vietnam from the French Empire. When the Japanese occupation began, the Viet Minh opposed Japan with support from the United States and the Republic of China. After the Second World War the Viet Minh opposed the re-occupation of Vietnam by France and continued a campaign of armed resistance. They were short on modern military knowledge and created a military school in Tinh Quang Ngai in 1946.

More than four hundred Vietnamese were trained by Japanese soldiers, becoming the hard core of a new military movement fighting for the liberation of Indochina from the French. French General Jean-Etienne Valluy quickly pushed the Viet Minh out of Hanoi when his infantry, supported by armoured units, re-took Hanoi fighting small battles against isolated Viet Minh groups. The French encircled the Viet Minh base, Viet Bac, in 1947 but failed to defeat the Viet Minh forces and had to retreat soon after. The newly Communist People's Republic of China gave the Viet Minh both sheltered bases and heavy weapons with which to fight the French. With the additional weapons, the Viet Minh were able to take control over many rural areas of the country. Soon after that, they began to advance towards the French occupied areas.

"We…" His voice tailed off as a screech of static, followed by the piercing howl of feedback, sliced through his words. There were more clicks and static, then he continued.

"We invite you to lay down your arms. Your officers are just lackeys of the French government. Come to us, we will provide you with money and passage home."

Avril turned to look at his men. They were listening with avid fascination to the Commissar's words, but he was not unduly worried. They had seen the Viets' treatment of prisoners too often to be tempted into taking up the offer to surrender. Better to die quickly in battle than to suffer a long lingering death, hacked to shreds with your balls stuffed into your mouth.

"Private Chevaux," Avril called, "come over here. Do you think you could take him at this distance?"

Chevaux had advertised in the French military newspaper Caravelle for this posting, a system at that time unique to France.

'Private, Infantry Regt., sharpshooter, Saigon. Seeks exchange Mobile Group North Vietnam. Reply PO Box 269, Caravelle'.

The reply had come quickly from an overweight, over-aged private who was happy to swap the rough and tumble of service in a mobile group operating close to the Central Highland, for a more peaceful end to his service career in the backwater of Saigon. Chevaux seized the chance to practice his first love, long range sniping. He had become a valued and deadly member of the Second Parachute Battalion, part of the Elite Mobile Two.

Chevaux ran over to him, clutching his rifle. He was the Para's champion sharpshooter, a crack shot with the modified Springfield rifle he carried.

The M1903 Springfield, or more formally the United States Rifle, Calibre .30, Model 1903, was an American magazine-fed, 5-shot, bolt-action service rifle used primarily during the first half of the twentieth century. It was officially adopted as a United States military bolt-action rifle in 1905, and saw service in World War I. It was officially replaced as the standard infantry rifle by the faster-firing, semi-automatic eight round M1 Garand in 1937.

However, the M1903 Springfield remained in service as a standard issue infantry rifle during World War II, since the U.S.

entered the war without sufficient M1 rifles to arm all troops. It also remained in service as a sniper rifle during World War II, the Korean War and even in the early stages of the Vietnam War.

The 1903 rifle included a rear sight leaf that could be used to adjust for elevation. When the leaf was flat, the battle sight appeared on top. This sight was set for 546 yards and was not adjustable. When the leaf was raised it could be adjusted to a maximum extreme range of 2,875 yards. The rear sight could also be adjusted for windage. The 1903A3 rear sight was an aperture sight adjustable both for elevation and windage.

Chevaux used a custom rifle sight that had been machined for him by the base armourer, a keen shooter and precision engineer. His skill with the weapon was legendary.

He looked down at the man with the loudhailer.

"I think so, Lieutenant."

"Do it, Private. Show him the French brand of propaganda."

"Yes, Sir."

Chevaux, a half French half Vietnamese native of Saigon, lay down behind a low mound of earth and settled his rifle in a 'V' formed by two pieces of stone. He checked the wind, picking up a leaf from the ground and throwing it up in the air to check speed and direction. The other men watched, fascinated. It was a long shot, impossible for most men. But Chevaux was not most men. His shooting sometimes seemed to be more inspired by magic than technique.

Four hundred metres away, Min rambled on.

"For those of you who wish merely to go home, we will

provide first class flights back to your home country. You will receive a reward of five thousand dollars each to help you on your journey. All you need do is…"

"I'm ready," Chevaux said quietly.

"Do him," Avril said.

"To shoot your officers and…"

'Crack!' The bullet flew unerringly to its target. Min spun around, the loudhailer crescendoed with furious, whining feedback and then was shut off. The Viets milled around him, two soldiers rushed across with a stretcher and loaded him onto it, carrying him off into the jungle. The rest of the guerrillas could be seen angrily gesturing up to the hilltop.

"A shoulder wound, I'm afraid," Chevaux apologised.

"But it shut him up, Private Chevaux. Well done, a magnificent shot. I owe you a bottle of Scotch when we get back to Hanoi."

The soldiers nearby looked at their lieutenant glumly, there were more angry shouts and commands from below, the Viet Minh were anxious to avenge the wounding of their Commissar. The odds against the French were formidable. No one needed to say, 'If we get back to Hanoi.'

"They're coming, Sir," shouted a soldier.

From below them the shouts became battle cries, "Tien-Len", 'Forward!' as the Viet Minh began a desperate charge up the hill. Rifle and machine gun fire whizzed all around the French troops, the Viet Minh were blazing away with rifles and submachine guns as they ran at the vastly outnumbered French position.

"Single shots, men, single shots, make them count. Take

cover and open fire!"

Avril checked around him. His lookouts at the rear were watching sharply for an enemy assault from behind. He ducked down and began firing.

The French poured a withering fire down on the attackers. Precise aimed shots that sliced into the Vietnamese guerrillas sending scores of them tumbling to the ground, killed or wounded. But there were too many. For every man that fell another two took his place, charging forward yelling savagely, manically forcing their way forward to kill the hated French invaders. Avril heard a click as a nearby man ran out of ammunition, his firing pin falling on an empty chamber.

"Grenades, throw the grenades," he shouted.

Eleven soldiers stood each holding one of their last precious grenades, pins pulled, they flung them into the advancing horde. Two of the grenade throwers were thrown back by Viet bullets. Explosions and screams added an unearthly harmony to the savage din of battle. Body parts spiralled into to the air, smoke billowed, wounded screamed their last, but still they came.

"Fix bayonets!" Avril shouted.

His men snatched out the sharpened bayonets and clicked them to their rifles. The first of the Viet Minh hurtled over the lip of the hill and flung themselves on the French soldiers. Several men fired, others skewered the Viets with the bayonets. The situation was desperate.

"Form around me!" Avril shouted.

The survivors rushed to gather around him in a tight, defensive circle. Bullets smacked sickeningly into flesh as the

Viet Minh shot indiscriminately at the tightly packed group of French survivors. Then they charged into them. Avril holstered his pistol, snatched up a rifle and stabbed an oncoming guerrilla with the bayonet. The man screamed and went down, his guts spilling out onto the hilltop as the bayonet ripped his stomach apart.

Avril got his pistol out and checked the chamber. Two bullets! He would need one for himself, rather than be taken alive and suffer the tortured hell the Viet Minh meted out to their French prisoners.

Suddenly there was a lull in the fighting. The Viet Minh paused, startled by something he couldn't see. Avril was astonished, why didn't they finish it? Then an eerie cry rang across the hilltop.

"Deutschland!"

A German cry, out of place in this French colony of Vietnam. Then more cries.

"Vive la France, Allah Akbar!"

The shouts became louder and overlapped each other, so that he couldn't make out who was shouting what. Then a group of men charged across the top, they had come from the side of the hill away from the fighting. They were all shooting fast short, accurate bursts from the submachine guns they all carried. Mostly German MP40's, he noted with bemusement. Quick sharp commands were spat out in a mixture of French and German. Two machine gun squads deployed on the hilltop. Instantly the guns began firing more German weapons. The heavy, menacing, deep repetitive burst of the MG34's flinging the Viet Minh attackers to the ground in a bloody, mangled ruin.

They were legionnaires, he noted, French Foreign Legion. The Legion had a reputation in Vietnam as brave, hard fighting men. So much so that they were often sent into the thickest part of the battle, the most dangerous missions that chewed normal men up and spat them out.

But these were in a different league from any legionnaires Avril had seen before. They moved and fought with precision, commands obeyed instantly, men rushed forward, fired and dropped to reload. Their comrades rushed up behind them giving covering fire, it was magnificent. They were no more than about a half company, perhaps fifty men.

Hundreds of Viet Minh still milled around the hilltop, but they were already defeated. The new arrivals rushed at them, tearing into them with the machine like precision that was awe inspiring. The Viets turned and ran. Instantly, the legion sergeant in charge barked an order. Eight men rushed forward, unslinging their rifles as they ran. They reached the edge of the hilltop and began pouring their accurate rifle fire on the retreating men. Many fell. Some managed to reach the cover of the jungle and ran out of the deadly hail of rifle fire. Others crawled forward, wounded, trying to follow their comrades. One by one they were dispatched by the riflemen. Silence descended on the hill.

Avril stood frozen, numbed by the furious firefight, amazed to still be alive. The sergeant came up to him. Avril reached out and shook his hand.

"Thank you, Sergeant. You saved our lives, without question. We were finished."

"You're welcome, Lieutenant. Very welcome."

"Corporal," he shouted to one of his legionnaires. "Do we have any wounded? No? Good, get some help for the paras, some of them look hurt."

Avril looked again, and then blinked. The sergeant wore a death's head enamel badge pinned to his uniform. The lieutenant looked around, most of the other legionnaires also wore similar death's head insignia on their uniforms. Then he remembered the battle shouts, 'Deutschland'. What was that all about?

"You're Germans, yes? That badge. You're Nazis!"

"Sieg Heil," the sergeant replied, smiling broadly. "Ex-Nazis, actually, my friend. We're all on the same side now. Not all of us are German, we have some Vietnamese, Montagnards, hill fighters. Several North Africans, Muslims. Even men from the Ukraine and Russia, some of them are Orthodox Christians. But our biggest group by far is German."

"Wherever you're from, thank God you came," Avril replied.

He looked around at the legionnaires. They looked exceptionally tough, a group of hard, competent veterans. Their uniforms were a collection of official legion issue and personal items. Their equipment was similarly a mix of standard and non-standard. Most were festooned with bandoliers, hand grenades and each carried a sub machine gun, mostly the German MP40. They all looked hard, savage, but with an air of calm assurance. These were men who'd done this many, many times before. Savagely fallen on a foe many times their number and wiped them out through sheer force of hard precision soldiering, delivered with a vicious savagery that seemed calculated and confident. This savagery terrifying an enemy and without allowing their own emotions to impair their almost robotic, production line killing.

"Lieutenant, the monkeys will reform before long. Then they'll be back. They may even have mortars, we need to get off this hill."

"How did you find us?" Avril asked him.

"We were ordered to Mao Khe, General de Lattre has got wind of a big Viet force in the area. Our friend Giap is stirring up lots of trouble for us, it seems. We were heading for the town when we heard the shooting, so we detoured to take a look."

"Lucky for us you did. It's the first time I've been happy to meet a German with a machine gun," Avril smiled.

"I'm Lieutenant Avril, Andre Avril, 6th Colonial Parachute Battalion."

"And I'm Sergeant Jurgen Hoffman, Sir. A Company, 2nd Battalion, 13th Half Brigade, Foreign Legion."

"And before the Foreign Legion, Sergeant?"

Hoffman stared at him. Then he grinned.

"Waffen-SS, Das Reich, Panzer Infantry. My rank was SS-Sturmbannführer. Is that a problem for you, Lieutenant?"

"Not at all, Sergeant, what's done is done. We're all damn grateful to you and your men. What next, do you think?"

They were interrupted by a whistling sound. A mortar shell arced high in the sky then descended towards them.

"Down!" shouted Hoffman.

He grabbed Avril and flung him to the ground. The shell exploded just past the crest of the hill, showering them with dirt and foliage, but there were no casualties.

Hoffman leapt to his feet and began shouting orders, "Grab your equipment, check your weapons men. Point men, we're going out the way we came in. Move out, go, go!"

"Lieutenant, get your men ready, I suggest you march in the middle of my unit. We'll hand out spare ammunition on the way, let's go."

Avril stood open mouthed for a moment. He was a paratrooper, a lieutenant in the elite of the French army, indeed, the elite of any army. This legionnaire sergeant was like a whirlwind rushing him along, with no time for planning, consultation, and command decisions.

"Sergeant, should we not..."

Another mortar shell slammed into the hilltop, they managed to drop flat but two of Avril's men were too slow, still on their feet when it landed. The metal fragments sliced through them, leaving butchered pieces of flesh flying through the air.

"Whatever it is, Lieutenant, save it for later. We're going. Move out!"

The point men were already halfway down the reverse side of the hill, machine gunners were covering them against any possible ambush. Hoffman's sharpshooters covered the Viet Minh positions, firing when any of them dared to show his face out of the jungle in possible preparation for an attack. Avril could see two corporals pushing his own men into position in the centre of the Foreign Legion column. Then Hoffman grabbed him. "Come, Lieutenant. Our place is at the front, that's the way we do it in the Legion. In the Waffen-SS too," he laughed.

The two commanders, Sergeant and Lieutenant, ran to the front of the column and began trekking down the hill, their men following. As soon as they reached the bottom the machine gunners joined the main group, then the sharpshooters. The rearguard joined them just as they were moving into the dark green foliage, out of sight of the hilltop which soon would be swarming with Viet Minh. They entered the jungle and followed a track that the legionnaires seemed to be familiar with, marching on for two kilometres. Seeing Avril glancing around him, Hoffman explained.

"This path leads to Mao Khe, Lieutenant. General de Lattre invited us to join him there. I've ordered our quartermaster to supply your men with fresh ammunition. I trust you were headed to Mao Khe too?"

Avril was still stunned by the suddenness of the Viet Minh attack which could have been the end of his entire command, then the ferocious assault and rescue by these German led legionnaires.

"I will need to contact my HQ for further orders, Sergeant."

"Orders?" Hoffman looked puzzled.

"Were you not ordered to join the action at Mao Khe?"

"Yes, of course, but…" Avril was interrupted.

"Then that's where we're going. Keep moving, the Viets will already be looking for us."

The Sergeant pressed forward, leading a blistering pace. Avril could feel himself beginning to tire, but it would be embarrassing to admit it to this ex-Nazi. Then he heard a shout from his men.

"Sir, we've got two men down, both wounded. We need to

stop for a rest."

Avril shouted over to Hoffman.

"Sergeant, you heard, we need to take a break."

The German smiled at him.

"You take a break and you die, Lieutenant. The Viets will be up behind us. Do you want your men killed?"

Avril boiled over, he was greatly indebted to the Sergeant for their rescue, but he had wounded who needed tending to.

"No, but neither do I want my wounded to die from lack of basic medical care. We take a break, that's an order, Sergeant."

Hoffman shrugged, then turned and made a hand signal. Instantly his men deployed sharpshooters and machine gunners, rushing out to make guard points to the front and rear of the column.

"The Lieutenant ordered a rest, men. Keep sharp, the Viet Minh are all around us." He turned to look at Avril.

"What now, Sir?" he put an emphasis on the 'Sir'. Avril knew he was being mocked but the German's arrogance was irritating, besides his wounded did need attention.

Sergeant Hoffman wore a black 'Schiff', a German side cap popular in the Waffen-SS, instead of the regulation Foreign Legion beret. A complicated man, an unrepentant Nazi possibly, but a fine soldier. The lieutenant knew he was totally and utterly outclassed in military matters by what this SS veteran had demonstrated on the hilltop, but he was determined to show him that a Frenchman could be his equal. He went to his men and double checked their supplies. The legionnaires had replenished their ammunition during the march, they had enough bullets to fight with.

"Make sure the wounded can walk, Corporal. Give them as much help as they need, we'll be leaving shortly. You should…"

An outbreak of firing cut off his words. The Viet Minh had caught up and were attacking in strength.

Hoffman's machine guns had opened up, the rearguard catching the pursuing Viet Minh unawares. The heavy MG34's fired in quick short bursts and the answering screams an eloquent testimony to their deadly accuracy and rate of fire. Four sharpshooters went hurtling back to join them. Within seconds the crack of their measured, aimed shots added to the crescendo and chaos of the MG34's firing over the sound of the Viet Minh Soviet made SKS rifles, the chatter of the MAT 49's and home-made sten guns directly copied from the British design, that the Viets were using in increasing numbers.

At the start of the war, the Viet Minh didn't have the means to acquire weaponry in large quantities. Initially these hurdles were overcome by the use of looted weapons, stolen from the Japanese and later the French. Nationalist China provided some training facilities and weaponry during WW2 as part of the American-led scheme of anti-Japanese partisans. Much Japanese weaponry fell into Viet Minh hands during the confusion of the Japanese surrender in 1945.

Later, with the Communist victory in China of 1949, secure bases for training and weapon production could be placed beyond or close to the Chinese border with Tonkin. The quantity and diversity of Viet Minh weaponry increased steadily throughout the war, as did the skill with which this material was distributed, and the training standards of the regular troops.

The VM readily produced numerous clandestine arms workshops throughout Vietnam. They also established a hidden factory in Thailand and others just across the Chinese border in Yunnan. These eventually produced rifles, SMGs, grenades, ammunition, mortars, RCLs, bazookas, mines, Bangalore Torpedoes and other explosive devices. The first factories were set up to produce the relatively simple British Sten gun, using machinery and material either bought or stolen. During 1946-47 these workshops produced around 30,000 Sten guns. Less than accurate at anything other than short range fighting, they were devastating in the sudden surprise attacks frequently encountered by French forces in Indochina

"We need to move, Lieutenant, it seems your rest has been terminated by our monkey friends."

Avril shrugged off Hoffman's arrogant, goading remark. It was true they needed to move fast to get away from these marauding guerrillas snapping at their heels, and rejoin the main French forces that were facing Giap at Mao Khe. He shouted to his men.

"Move out."

Hoffman's legionnaires needed no orders. They were up and ready to move, in a strong mobile defensive formation.

"Let's go," Hoffman shouted.

For the next thirty minutes they fought a running battle. Avril was astounded at the speed and professionalism of these Foreign Legion fighters. Their style of fighting looked somehow familiar, then he realised where he'd seen it before. In old German wartime newsreels, when he was a young man in occupied France. The Germans were always keen to show off the prowess of their conquering armies.

What he was seeing was the very embodiment of a Waffen-SS fighting unit engaged in a running battle, fast, hard hitting, with the unit commander leading from the front. Hoffman had trained his men to fight as an SS unit, attacking where the enemy was strongest. Avril noted that Hoffman himself seemed to be everywhere at once, joining the machine gunners and sharpshooters to check their progress and constantly monitoring their positions, the men and the equipment.

It was not the French way, where a degree of separation was usually considered correct between the officers, NCO's and men. The officer gave orders to a subordinate structure of sergeants and corporals who passed his wishes on to the men. Now, the SS style of fighting had arrived in Vietnam. Perhaps they were needed, reflected Avril. Without them his command would have been overrun.

The previous year Giap's forces had torn apart the French defenders along Route Coloniale 4, following the retreat from Cao Bang, giving them virtually the keys to the whole of Northern Tonkin, the far north of the country.

The Battle of Cao Bang was an ongoing campaign in northern Indochina during the Indochina War, between the French Far East Expeditionary Corps and the Viet Minh, which began in October 1947 and ended in September 1949.

Since the start of the conflict, Viet Minh troops had ambushed French convoys along the Vietnam-China border from the Gulf of Tonkin on a hundred and forty seven mile route to a French garrison at Cao Bang, known as Route Colonial 4, or RC4. Repeated ambushes led to French operations of increasing strength to reopen the road, including a costly mission by the Foreign Legion in February 1948.

On July 25th, 1948, the Cao Bang encampment was itself attacked and held out for three days with two companies defending against two battalions of Viet Minh. A further twenty eight ambushes took place in 1948.

In February 1949, five Viet Minh battalions and mortar units took a French post at Lao Cai, and resumed ambushes through the monsoon season.

On September 3rd, 1949, one hundred vehicles left That Khe in a reinforced convoy on a sixteen mile drive through infantry screens. The French, reduced to one soldier per vehicle due to troop numbers, were ambushed by automatic fire. The first twenty trucks were halted, as were the final ten, and the middle of the convoy was cut down by shellfire. The following day French troops reoccupied the surrounded hilltops, however only four French wounded were found alive.

The campaign at Cao Bang resulted in a change in convoy practices for the remainder of the war. Vehicles now travelled from post to post in ten to twelve vehicle convoys, through security screens of French troops and with aircraft observation. In 1950 supply convoys to Cao Bang were discontinued in favour of air supply.

Giap had tried to repeat his recent stunning victory at Vinh Yen, but this time his troops were routed by the French. Now he was trying again to defeat the French in a major action at Mao Khe. The Vietnamese guerrillas seemed to be everywhere at once, sniping and ambushing the colonial forces almost at will.

Avril shuddered for even thinking it, he was the victim of the brutal Nazi conquerors in his own native land of France. Yet here he was on the opposite side, it was the French who were the colonial conquerors, fighting a desperate action to try and contain the communists. With men like Hoffman, and his SS-trained legionnaires, it would certainly make a difference.

He laughed to himself, imagining telling the French High Command to adopt SS fighting tactics. That would be the end of his career. He might just find himself in charge of a barracks storeroom outside of Marseille. He heard a shout ahead, they were nearing the edge of the jungle. In the distance he could see the buildings of Mao Khe. There was a tricolour flag on a pole. Thank God, the French were still in command of the town.

As abruptly as they had appeared, the Viet Minh who'd dogged their heels during the withdrawal from the hilltop retreated back into the jungle, their noses bloodied by Hoffman's incisive and determined rear guard defence.

No more French troops had been hit, yet the legionnaires estimated the enemy casualties at around eighty or ninety. Avril had no reason to doubt it, a stunning result, and now they had rejoined the main army.

They marched into the town, saluting the flag as they went past.

"I must leave you now, Lieutenant," Hoffman said.

"My unit is camped the other side of the town. I wish you good luck."

He held out his hand. Avril took it.

"Thank you, Sergeant Hoffman."

34

"You are very welcome, my friend," he smiled, sardonically. "A little compensation from the Reich, Ja?"

"Fuck you," Avril replied, but he smiled to take the sting out of the words as he walked away.

He found the headquarters of the 6th Colonial Parachute Battalion and went to report on his unit action and casualties, including the death of their commander, Captain Balmain. A full colonel sat at a folding table, pouring over maps of the area. Avril made his report, including the part played by Hoffman's legionnaires.

"He seemed to know what his was doing, this Sergeant Hoffman," Avril told the colonel.

The colonel goggled at him.

"Seemed to know? Hoffman? You don't know him? He's a superb soldier, Lieutenant. He's still only a sergeant because of the rules in the Legion that uniquely allow only Frenchmen to be officers."

"Yes, he told me he was German, a member of the Waffen-SS during the war."

The colonel smiled at him.

"That's true. Hoffman's not his real name, so I understand. Like most former SS men, he took an assumed name when he joined the Legion. You know that after 1947 our government prohibited any former SS being recruited into the Legion, but by that time of course, many had already joined."

"How did they know who was SS and who was not?" Avril asked.

"By the tattoo, Lieutenant, the blood type tattoo under the armpit that almost all SS recruits were required to have. The idea was that if they were wounded in battle they would get matching blood in the event a transfusion was needed. When the war turned against Germany many SS recruits declined the tattoo, especially when it became known that SS soldiers taken prisoner were subjected to terrible torture. So many recruits in the Legion were unknown to us as former SS."

"I see. Well, Hoffman is certainly a good man in a fight."

"Good?" The Colonel's smile broadened.

"Yes, he is good. He apparently joined the Waffen-SS in the ranks as a private soldier. He was commissioned quite early on, after destroying two Soviet tanks singlehanded on the Eastern Front, using hand held Panzerfausts. He once showed me the tank destroyer badges, Hoffman earned a total of five before the war ended. He holds the Iron Cross First Class with Oak Leaves for bravery, heaven knows how many lesser medals, wound badges, campaign medals, cuff titles, you name it and he was there! He reached the rank of Sturmbannführer, that's equivalent to Major, before his wounds took him out of the battlefield just before the war ended. He ended up in a French POW camp, from where he was recruited to the Legion. He was one of the most highly decorated soldiers in his regiment, SS Das Reich. Our commanders here turned a blind eye when the government banned ex-SS volunteers, they flatly refused to throw him out. You were lucky he came to your aid. The Viets know of him, of course, they have a price on his head. I believe it currently stands at ten thousand United States dollars."

"I can see why they would want him dead," said Avril.

"Indeed, Lieutenant. Indeed. Now, I suggest you attend to your men, General de Lattre expects the offensive to begin at any time, Giap has been building his reinforcements in the area for several days. I suspect we'll be very busy."

"Yes, Sir." They exchanged salutes and Avril went off to organise his men.

They needed fresh supplies, weapons, ammunition, food and of course a radio to replace the one smashed in the Viet Minh assault.

Three hours later with only a small part of his resupply efforts completed, the Viet Minh struck with both artillery and infantry, flinging themselves against the French troops in massed human wave assaults. They were, indeed, going to be very busy.

CHAPTER TWO

I watched the Lieutenant walk away, he looked tired, dangerously tired. Worse still, he looked beaten. I wondered how he would have fared on the Eastern Front, fighting another communist enemy, the savage hordes of Stalin's Soviet Union.

That was a war beyond the worst nightmares of man. A war against an enemy that, no matter how many were killed, seemed to have the limitless capacity to regenerate itself. Knock out a tank, two or three more appeared. Mow down a company of advancing Soviet infantry, a regiment appeared in its place. It seemed to be a communist philosophy that life was cheap, able to be sacrificed as recklessly as its commanders wished, in both wartime and peacetime alike.

Our mission here was the same as in Russia. Kill the enemy, nothing more. Slaughter them so that they couldn't be patched up and pitched back into the battle. Terrify them with a violent ferocity that was calculated to keep them awake long into the reaches of the night.

The communists shared the same philosophy, it was true, a campaign of limitless violence calculated to murder and terrorise all who opposed them.

But theirs was a war with a difference. We begrudged every man who fell in battle, every death and every casualty. Our tactics were based on preserving the lives of the men at any cost. The communists just spent the lives of their troops as if each man had the value of a piece of confetti, tossed at a village wedding, no more value than a useless, discarded piece of coloured paper. Their civilians were fair game too, human slaves to be exploited, threatened, tortured and killed if they failed to obey their masters. Eventually, this war would be decided not by the side that killed the most enemy, there were just too many soldiers on each side to simply kill them all. It would be decided by the army that either convinced the civilians to resist the terror or forced them to submit to it. That freedom was worth fighting for. Slavery was a living death in itself.

"Jurgen, you've got problems of the world on your shoulders!" a cheery voice called over to me.

It was my good friend in the Legion, Captain Jacques Legrand.

"Jacques," I replied, happy to see the young captain. We shook hands, although several years younger than me, Legrand was always happy to listen to the voices of more experienced men, officers or not. Unlike the regular French troops, the Legion in Vietnam had much of the easy formality that I had been used to in the Waffen-SS. He handed me a cigarette, took one himself as we chatted about our next mission. A tall, handsome and accomplished young man, he always seemed to have the most attractive girls in the bar competing to be on his arm. Or in his bed. But when he was on duty, he was the complete professional. I focussed on what he was saying.

"What's going on?"

"The brass expects Giap to launch an attack at any moment. Artillery are all standing by for fire orders, the air force are running back to back missions reconnoitring the enemy positions and waiting for a chance to unload their bombs on to the heads of our local communists. Are your men ready to deploy, I don't think we've got much time left to us? I gather you were involved in some kind of a skirmish outside the town, do you need time to re-equip and regroup?"

I shook my head.

"It was nothing big. Sergeant Petrov is drawing ammunition from the stores right now. No casualties, we just need time to catch our breath and we'll be ready to fight."

"Good. I've got some beer in the tent, do you want one?"

"Another time, Jacques," I smiled. "What's the intelligence on the enemy forces?"

"Not good. Three divisions, 308, 312 and the 316. In total, they've got at least ten thousand men, possibly even more."

"And us? What's our strength?"

"Apart from the Legion, we've got Colonial paratroops and infantry. A Senegalese unit, the 30th. Several armoured cars, some Tho partisan units."

"Partisans?" I spat out.

I hated partisans. A large part of my time in Russia had been spent slaughtering the irregulars that infiltrated our lines and caused such havoc and fear to the regular troops. They were like lice, when you felt the itch and discovered them amongst you, you killed them.

"Yes, I know the record of the Waffen-SS in Russia," he laughed, "but these people really hate the communists. They're good fighters too. De Lattre also arranged for some gunboats on the river, the Da Bach. They'll give us useful artillery support. We're outnumbered, of course, even allowing for the Viet Minh we don't yet know about, but we're better equipped and better prepared. We'll blow them back to the stone age," he grinned.

"It sounds good, in theory, Jacques. Let's see how it goes in practice. I need to rejoin my men, we'll join you shortly."

We exchanged salutes and I went off to find my company office, where I received orders to report to the captain on the defensive perimeter of Mao Khe. The whole town was a hubbub of military preparation. French Colonial infantry and paratroopers, Senegalese, their black faces striking and incongruous, Vietnamese and part-Vietnamese, a mix of languages and troops. Foreign Legion, speaking French, Viet, German, Russian and Ukrainian, even some languages I'd never heard before in my life. Officers and Sergeants shouted commands, corporals chivvied their men into assigned places.

Hard eyed madams watched them all bustling past their brothels, calculating how many would be alive by tomorrow, how much could they charge? The girls watched from the balconies, trying to catch the eye of any soldier that took their fancy. A French soldier meant a passport out of this war ravaged country to the real or imagined luxuries of Paris. If you could persuade them to marry you. Some did. It meant clothes, good restaurants, theatre and social life. And of course security, the security that comes from knowing one's country is not being torn apart by a vicious and bloody civil war. The security that comes from knowing that the door will not be smashed down at midnight by a gang of drunken soldiers or a band of fanatical Viet Minh seeking revenge on women who dared to sell their bodies to the hated French colonialists.

I found my unit sitting in the sun outside a Vietnamese native bar. I didn't have to worry about drunkenness, thankfully. These men were professionals and needed no lessons in the value of keeping a clear head to fight the enemy. And win. My NCO's were all ex-SS. Not a result of deliberate racial discrimination, but discrimination nonetheless. I had trained my unit, with the permission of my commander, to fight the SS way. Our tactics were simple, the brutally hard application of maximum force, designed to shock and intimidate the enemy, giving us time to kill as many of them as possible while they were still gathering their wits. It only worked when the whole unit moved and fought as one man. Endless training, drills, ruthless discipline, and a strong esprit-de-corps were the ingredients that mixed together made us what we were. An elite fighting unit, respected by our superiors, hated and feared by the Viet-Minh. I needed experienced men to make it work, men who had fought and bled across the battlefields of Europe, practising the ruthless SS way of fighting that particular war.

They nodded a greeting as I walked up to them. My four NCO's sat relaxed, waiting to hear the unit orders. They were Corporal Karl-Heinz Vogelmann, a lean, hard veteran of SS

Das Reich, he had fought in Russia as well as many other of the European battlegrounds. Corporal Manfred von Kessler, the unit clown, invariably smiling and cracking jokes, his short, tubby appearance hid the reality of the man inside. Ex-SS Liebstandarte Adolf Hitler, von Kessler was a ruthless killer when needed. Sergeant Paul Schuster, ex-SS Totenkopf and Senior Sergeant Friedrich Bauer, lean, almost cadaverous, another veteran of SS-Liebstandarte Adolf Hitler. They were all veterans of the battlefields of Kursk, the Demyansk Pocket and many other Russian theatres, Greece, the Balkans, France, and finally the bloody struggle for Germany, Berlin, and the heart of the Reich itself.

Like me, they had acquired literally dozens of decorations, tank destroyer badges, wound badges, Iron Crosses and campaign cuff titles. Also like me they had opted to join the French Foreign Legion at a time when the future for Waffen-SS veterans looked bleak. Even before we left school we were playing soldiers in the Hitler Youth. Then the war arrived and changed our lives forever. Adolf Hitler's colossal, cruel miscalculation, surely the biggest lie any leader had ever inflicted on his people, with the exception of Joseph Stalin of course. And our local warlord, Ho Chi Minh was doing his best to get to the top of the blood soaked dictator ladder.

So here we were, Hitler's orphans, rootless, homeless, still fighting wars on foreign soil. At least we'd become good at what we did. Not all had learned quickly enough, but they were buried in the soil of Indochina, the forgotten men of ill-fated colonial conquests.

The men sat there smoking and chatting, laughing at another of von Kessler's jokes. Two girls were with hem, Mai St Martin, Vogelmann's pretty Eurasian girlfriend, and Thien van Hoc, von Kessler's equally beautiful Vietnamese native girl. The girls usually stayed near our base in Hanoi, but on this mission had accompanied the main force to this town of Mao Khe which was supposedly safe. Once again, our blundering intelligence officers had led us blindly into a dangerous battle zone that threatened to overwhelm us.

"Have you come to tell us about a week's leave we have been awarded, Jurgen?" my Senior Sergeant Friedrich Bauer asked me.

They all laughed, Giap had begun to throw in huge numbers of troops in the surrounding areas, well equipped divisions of hardened veterans. He was looking to build on his Cao Bang victory, there would be no leave for us, not in the foreseeable future.

"We're here to man a defensive perimeter around the town, reports show that the enemy are preparing to attack in strength." I showed them the map.

"Our company has been ordered here, Captain Leforge is already there with the rest of our company. We are to report there to him directly. Get the men together, latest intelligence places the Viets already massing just outside the town. An attack is certainly imminent."

"So the monkeys are swinging through the jungle towards us, are they?" Vogelmann grinned.

The corporal had a black eye patch and a ragged beard to hide the injuries he sustained when a tank shell came too close to his foxhole, his men called him 'Blackbeard'. He was also a fan of the new 'Tarzan' films that he'd seen in the cinema in Germany before the collapse. He came to Indochina expecting to see men in leotards swinging through the jungle on vines, dragging their attractive female mates along with them. We were certain he was still looking. In the meantime he regarded the Viet Minh as no higher up the scale than monkeys, a label many of us here gave to the ugly and brutal men that fought for the communist leader Ho Chi Minh.

"Indeed they are, Karl-Heinz, if you don't get out of that chair pretty damn quickly and pick up your weapons, they'll catch you sleeping and singe your arse."

There was a roar of laughter at Vogelmann's expense, but the nudge to get him into action was unnecessary. They were already getting up, checking their weapons and packs and preparing to rejoin the company. Suddenly, a mortar bomb whistled overhead and landed the other side of the town with a tremendous crash spurring the bustle of troops preparing for the coming battle to move faster.

Friedrich Bauer looked thoughtful for a moment.

"I reckon about two kilometres away, Jurgen. That was a heavy mortar. About thirty minutes before they hit us?"

"Agreed," I replied. "Come on. Let's get a nice SS welcome ready for Vogelmann's monkey friends, we need to move fast. Vogelmann, von Kessler, get the girls moving, there's a supply convey returning to Hanoi in the next hour, make sure they're on it."

They needed no more urging, we double-timed to our positions, whilst more mortar shells began landing around us. It wasn't a good sign, heavy mortars meant that for once our intelligence had got it right, these were well equipped and trained Viet Minh forces. We would have a battle on our hands.

We saluted Captain Jean Leforge and he returned the salutes.

"We have at least three divisions of Viet Minh expected to hit us shortly. As soon as their positions are confirmed, the artillery will start hitting them. We've also got the gunboats on the river waiting for fire orders. Our job is simple, we're moving forward to meet them, give them a bloody nose, they won't be expecting opposition before they reach the town. Get your men ready, we move out in ten minutes."

A runner came up with messages for him, so we left the Captain and went to check in with our men.

Sergeant Petrov greeted me, another veteran of the Eastern front, except that he fought for the Russians. Short, slight, with dark hair, a pointed beard and wire framed glasses, he was the very image of the unfortunate Leon Trotsky, murdered by Joseph Stalin. Cut off from his unit, the Second Shock Army, he was taken prisoner by the Wehrmacht and spent the rest of the war in a camp. Nikolai Petrov had survived the prison camp to be repatriated to Stalin's Russia, only to be branded a traitor for having been captured by the Nazis. Facing a lengthy term in a Siberian Gulag, Nikolai Petrov had jumped a train heading west, eventually winding up in France where he was recruited by the Legion. Strangely, he too had fought at Kursk, where many of our Waffen-SS recruits had fought. Had they ever exchanged shots, I wondered? Perhaps a question best not asked. Petrov carried out the job of quartermaster, when he was not engaged in what he was best at, the job of killing.

In the field he hunted down the Vietnamese partisans with all the brutality and dedication of the most ruthless SS-Partisan-jaeger, the German partisan hunters who operated behind the lines to hunt down and exterminate Russian guerrillas.

"Jurgen, we're ready to move, everyone is carrying their maximum load of weapons and ammunition. Food and water for two days, if we haven't done the job by then we'll not need any more than that."

I agreed, we should be out and back within twenty four hours. We simply had to hit the enemy hard and fast, our speciality. Hit their forward reconnaissance units, try and disrupt their command and control and generally inspire a healthy amount of fear in the Viet Minh. That would slow their advance, so that we would have time to bring the artillery into play and shred their slant eyed fanatics into a million pieces. That, at least, was the theory.

"Thanks, Nikolai." I checked my watch. "Five minutes, then we move."

I joined Captain Leforge, the company commander. He was a graduate of the École Spéciale Militaire de Saint-Cyr, the French equivalent of the American West Point or British Sandhurst officer training schools.

The French elite military academy was founded in Fontainebleau in 1803 by Napoleon Bonaparte near Paris in the buildings of the Maison Royale de St-Louis, a school founded in 1685 by Louis XIV for impoverished daughters of noblemen who had died for France. The cadets moved several times more, eventually settling in Saint-Cyr, located west of Paris, in 1808. They left the school with the rank of lieutenant and joined the specialist centre for their chosen branch for one additional year, before being assigned to a regiment to serve as a platoon leader. Like his illustrious French predecessor Napoleon Bonaparte, Leforge had intended joining the Artillery, the pride of the French army.

Unlike Napoleon, he didn't make it that far. A bully went too far in the Military College and Leforge's good friend was left with a fractured skull after the bully, one of the instructors, went too far in meting out punishment. Leforge went straight for the man to eke out revenge, breaking two of the bully's legs and one of his arms in the process. Rough justice had no place in the stiff, tradition-ruled French army, and it was made crystal clear that the regular army had no place for him. And so he entered the Foreign Legion, where he soon found a place for his brand of unconventional soldiering in the steaming jungles of South-East Asia, leading his elite company of hardened troops, all survivors of the most brutal battlefields the world had yet seen.

"Move out," Leforge shouted down the line.

Instantly our reconnaissance patrol went forward, a section of four men led by Corporal Manfred von Kessler. They travelled five hundred metres ahead of the main force and were lightly equipped and armed. Their packs and equipment were shared out amongst the men so that they only carried MP40 submachine guns with them, with the exception of Private Jean-Claude Armand, who carried a silenced Kar 98 sniper rifle.

Their job was to be our eyes and ears. If they ran into a Viet Minh main force, their only defence would be to see them before they were seen themselves and then rejoin the company as quickly as possible. They disappeared into the dark greenery of the jungle. Then Leforge signalled us to follow.

We travelled for only a kilometre before von Kessler brought his men back hurriedly.

"We have company," he told Leforge, who waited with me and the other Sergeants.

"Viet Minh battalion, I'd guess, certainly more than five hundred men. They're grouped up ahead, about half a kilometre from here, the trail is totally blocked."

"No way around them?"

"None."

"Very well," Leforge said, "we'll give them a bloody nose. That's what we're here for, to disrupt their attack, so if we can get these monkeys running, maybe they'll make the rest think twice about staying. Hoffman, any suggestions?"

I thought for a moment. The odds were high, at least five hundred Viet Minh and only a hundred of us. But we had the advantage of surprise. We were undoubtedly more heavily armed, and had absorbed the lessons of many battles where the odds were stacked against us.

"They must be preparing to move, the attack is undoubtedly building right now. I suggest we prepare an ambush right here, mine the track, we can detonate it as they come past then, open up with everything we've got. That should do it, but if they get any warning that we're here it won't work. Then we'll have a real fight on our hands."

"Agreed, Sergeant Hoffmann. We'll make damn sure they

don't get wind of our presence. Senior Sergeant Bauer, Sergeant Schuster," he called, "pass the word, make preparations for the ambush right here, and if anyone makes a sound when they're in position, I'll gut them personally. Clear?"

"Sir."

Bauer and Schuster doubled away to get the men into position.

"Sergeant Hoffmann, get your explosives man to mine the path, we may not have much time."

"Yes, Sir," I replied then went to find Petrov.

Nikolai Petrov was a man of many talents, learned on the battlefields of the Eastern Front, then honed to perfection in the jungle hell of Indochina. One of his talents was with explosives. He had the instinct to know exactly how much explosive was required for a particular job, never too much, never too little. He also had the cunning to know how to disguise his deadly charges, making them all but impossible to detect. Until it was too late, of course.

"Petrov, we need this track mined, several hundred Viet Minh so we'll need staged charges along a section of track, say two hundred metres? Do you have enough charges?"

"That will be twenty charges at ten metre intervals. I think we have about fifteen charges with us, that'll make about fourteen metre intervals. It should do it, Jurgen."

"Very well, get it done. I'll get the men deployed."

I went and deployed my section, fifty men, all heavily concealed with criss-crossing fields of fire. The last thing I needed was 'friendly fire casualties'. I could see Senior Sergeant Bauer doing the same thing with the other half of the company. Captain Leforge was on the radio to headquarters, calling in details of the Viet Minh location. I did the rounds of my men.

"When the mines explode, usual drill, hit them with everything we've got. I want grenades hitting them, semi-automatic fire, I want to see those MP40's earning their keep. You know how it goes, no time for niceties, kill the bastards. Vogelmann, how are the MG42's looking, any problems?"

"All set, Jurgen, just waiting for business."

I checked the heavy machine guns. We had eight in the company, four in my section, and four in Bauer's. A lot of firepower for a mere company, but we found the nuisance of carrying them around the jungle was more than outweighed by the devastating effect of multiple heavy machine guns opening fire unexpectedly on the slant eyed monkeys. I could just make out two of the tips of the barrels, the other two were totally invisible, but the enemy wouldn't see them until it was too late.

"Good, Karl-Heinz, just watch the crossfire," I warned him.

He looked at me reproachfully. He'd learned his trade in the SS-Liebstandarte Adolf Hitler. From the Russian Front to the final offensives in Western Europe, then surviving in Indochina for more than five years, he wasn't about to make mistakes.

"Good." I went to find Leforge.

"We're all set, Captain."

"Good, get in position, it shouldn't be long."

I walked into the jungle foliage and took up position with my troops. I wasn't unduly worried. We'd done this many times before, although a company up against at least a battalion was high odds, high enough to make me cautious. We waited, the minutes dragged by. I started to get nervous, the slightest noise would alert the Viet Minh and we couldn't survive a prolonged firefight.

But we were professionals, doing our job, the job we had trained for. Some of us thousands of miles away in the snowy wastes of the Soviet Union, in the forests of the Ardennes, or the ruined cities of Germany, bombed by the RAF and US Air Force, shelled and machine gunned by the Allied forces as they crushed the mighty German war machine.

There was no noise. No one smoked to give the game away. No one spoke, even murmured. We were all well aware of the high stakes on which our lives, and the lives of our comrades, rested.

Then I heard it, initially a slight noise, just a disturbance in the natural rhythm of the jungle. It was the gentle footfalls of hundreds of men, moving stealthily along the path. I heard the odd snatch of whispered conversation. They were confident, so confident to be whispering to each other and that they hadn't even put point men to provide forward reconnaissance. The arrogant bastards, I thought. They may think they own this patch of jungle, but they haven't won it yet.

Then they came into view. They were Viet Minh regulars, wearing the distinctive beige uniform with the upturned conical hats. They carried an assortment of weapons, Mauser rifles, German war surplus, like our MP40's and MG42's. Soviet made PPSh submachine guns with stick magazines, more suited to light, mobile jungle warfare than the more traditional pancake magazine commonly used on the Eastern Front. Some of the regulars carried Russian Moisin Nagant rifles, others were carrying captured French and British equipment, including the familiar Lee Enfield Mark 4. In the middle of the line of Viet Minh walked their officers and commissars, all of whom were distinguished by their headgear, a collection of trilby type hats and forage caps. Each of them, unlike their men, carried a holstered pistol, whilst the men carried heavy rucksacks. It was as if the officers and commissars disdained to wear the headgear of the common soldier. Which they probably did, the message of Marxist equality was strictly for the peasants.

In reality Ho Chi Minh's new Vietnam was rather different, it reminded me in many ways of Adolf Hitler's Germany. They had their versions of the Gestapo, the SS, and the SD. Elections were regarded as something of a fairy story. Adolf would have been quite at home amongst these people.

They were indeed at battalion strength, the leading men had almost gone past our hidden mines while the end of the line had still to come into view. Leforge judged it would have to be enough. He was crouched near to me and I saw his hand signal to Petrov. Almost immediately there was a series of massive explosions, the peaceful sounds of the forest were ripped apart by the noise. Thousands of birds took to the skies in a whistling, twittering swarm, hurriedly escaping man's destructive folly.

There was a short pause, I could only hear slight background noises. Then tons of debris thrown up by the blast settled down over us.

Amidst the cries of agony from the wounded Viets our men opened up. Grenades sailed over the jungle foliage, to land in the middle of the human devastation. So far, not a shot had been fired in return. Then I heard the heavy bursts of machine gun fire as the MG42's began sending their message of death. The fire was punctuated by the lighter bursts of submachine gun fire from the MP40's. In the distance I could hear the crack, crack, as our sharpshooters picked off targets of opportunity, enemy soldiers who thought themselves lucky to have escaped the blast, fleeing down the track only to be struck down by our snipers. I could just make out Private Armand hidden in the fork made by two trees, invisible to the Viets on the path, firing shot after aimed shot at those who survived and tried to flee. He seemed to never miss. There would be a distinctive high crack that rose above the din of the machine guns and grenades. A man would throw up his arms and tumble over, then another crack, another man dead, and on it went, machine-like killing.

Eventually Leforge shouted for ceasefire and sent our reconnaissance patrol further up the path to check for any remaining Viets.

The jungle was quiet, eerily so, after the shattering noise of our gunfire. We picked our way carefully out of the jungle to check the casualties. We had to be careful, some fanatics would feign death to get a shot at the hated white colonialists. We had a simple rule, if in doubt, kill the bastards. I used my pistol to put a bullet in a Viet I thought I saw moving, his head twitched to the side as my bullet took him in the back of his brain, and then he lay still. All along the path our men were despatching other survivors of our attack, wounded or not. The occasional shot rang out, a scream, a groan.

One Viet Minh, a commissar by the look of him, took a grenade from a dead comrade next to him and went to throw it, propping himself up with one arm in his agony, determined to inflict pain on the colonialist enemy. Senior Sergeant Bauer was nearby, watching carefully, the battlefield strewn with bodies was nothing new to him. He saw the movement, rushed over and threw the body of a dead Viet soldier on top of the grenade. There was a muted blast, pieces of the dead soldier sprayed the ground, leaving the commissar staring stupidly at his bloody shoulder. The dead body had protected all but his arm, which had disappeared and left a bloody, bleeding stump. His screams echoed through the jungle, until Bauer casually finished him with a three shot burst from his MP40.

Our patrol came rushing back.

"Some of the Viet Minh escaped, there's a much bigger Viet force following the one we just shot up. They're coming straight towards us, we won't get a chance to ambush this lot, they're being very careful, point men both sides of the track," von Kessler reported to me and Leforge.

He was breathless, they had been running. What a damn nuisance, we'd used our mines and explosives on this action, we had no replacements. Leforge turned to me.

"Sergeant, I don't see any alternative but a withdrawal to Mao Khe. We can't hold off a division."

I agreed, we had done our job, and done it well, several hundred less Viet Minh to join the attack on Mao Khe.

"Form up," Leforge ordered, "we're pulling back now. Point men, move out."

Von Kessler took his four man squad and began retracing our steps back to Mao Khe. The main body of men were on their feet, packs and equipment loaded, weapons checked and ready for instant action.

"Corporal Vogelmann, take five other men to the rearguard, take two of the MG42's"

"Sir," Vogelmann instantly issued orders and raced to the back of the column with the five men and two MG42's, the heavy load spread between them.

Leforge said, "Jurgen, send your fastest two men back to our stores in the town, they're to bring back another batch of mines for Sergeant Petrov. If we've got time, we'll try mining the path nearer the town. They'll be careful, but so will we, and we may catch some of them again."

I went and detailed two men to dash back to get the explosives, and then I joined my men.

There was little talk. We'd all done this too many times before to discuss or question any orders. We survived this war by carrying out our missions with a dedicated professionalism, an unswerving attitude to battle that had carried us through many, many bloody fights where the amateurs and the careless had fallen to enemy fire and their own rank stupidity.

"Move out," Leforge shouted.

The column moved off, heading back to Mao Khe. We travelled back half a kilometre, with only another half kilometre between us and the town. Our two runners met us on the path, carrying packs loaded with mines, they had fourteen in all, as many as they could carry.

Petrov took over, preparing the load on the march, fitting fuses and preparing the explosives for use. He dropped out of the column with three men. They let us go past and then began preparing their charges. I could see Petrov fitting a charge in one of the bigger trees, a clever move. The Viets would be looking for freshly dug soil. While they watched the ground the charges at face level in the trees would detonate, hopefully blowing off more than a few of their communist ideas clean out of their heads.

He caught up with us just as we were entering Mao Khe.

"All set, Jurgen, we should catch a few of them."

As he spoke, there was a roar of explosions that rippled out of the jungle.

"Seems to have worked," he said with satisfaction. "That means they're only half a kilometre away."

"Yes, well done, Nikolai, go and join the men. The monkeys will be here soon looking for revenge."

He dashed off. Leforge had heard the explosion and was giving orders for the defence to be prepared.

"Radioman," he shouted, "get me our air liaison, I'll order up a Napalm strike on the area around that Viet division.

Napalm is a result of a gelling agent mixed with gasoline which we frequently used in military operations as a part of an incendiary weapon. It causes severe burns to the skin and body, asphyxiation, unconsciousness and death. One of the main features of was that it stuck well to the naked skin, and hence it left no real chance for removing the burning Napalm from the victim's skin. We normally used it against dug-in enemy personnel.

The burning incendiary composition flowed into foxholes, trenches, bunkers, drainage and irrigation ditches and other improvised troop shelters. In the killing fields of Indochina, it was a lethal killer, one of the most deadly, delivered by air it was normally devastating to a well dug in enemy.

"Jurgen," he said to me.

"I want an artillery strike to hit them hard, get on the field telephone. Call down an artillery strike on their estimated co-ordinates. If they want revenge, we'll give them a bit more to feel sore about. By the time they get over that lot, the air force will be over with their second course of Napalm."

I picked up a field telephone and got through to our artillery.

"Sorry, Sergeant," the artillery officer replied, "all our artillery has been ordered to engage other targets, we've got a lot of Viets inbound. Try the navy, they'll be glad to have your business."

I thanked him and got through to our ships, waiting off the coast. We had a Dinassaut on the nearby river, a unique French invention that was proving to be very successful in this type of war. Several surplus US tank landing craft, donated to the French by their American friends, were converted into gunboats with the addition of mortars and a range of heavy weaponry, it was a lot of firepower.

The Dinassaut, or Division d'Infanterie Navale d'Assaut, a Naval Assault Infantry Division, was a type of riverine military unit employed by the French Navy during the Indochina War. Each Dinassaut consisted of approximately twelve craft, the American landing craft modified with armour and using tank turrets as weapons. They used other craft carrying 81mm mortars to be employed as riverine artillery. Used effectively, it was a formidable weapon.

I gave the coordinates and left them to open fire as soon as possible. We'd done everything possible. We were well positioned for defence, well armed and supplied. We now had to wait for the next move. It wasn't the Viet Minh who made it, but the Air Force who arrived with two Grumman F8F Bearcats, swooping in over the town for their attack run.

The Bearcat concept was inspired by the early 1943 evaluation of a captured Focke-Wulf Fw 190 by Grumman test pilots and engineering staff. Compared to the earlier Hellcat, the Bearcat was lighter, had a much better rate of climb and was 50 mph faster. The F8F prototypes were ordered in November 1943 and first flew on 21 August 1944, nine months later. The first production aircraft was delivered in February 1945 and the first squadron was operational by May, but World War II was over before the aircraft saw combat service.

Our air force had bought many of the American fighters and used them effectively in the skies of Indochina. Although their range was somewhat limited, which made them less useful than they might have been. Armed with four 0.50 calibre machine guns or four 20mm M3 cannon, as well as four unguided rockets, the F8F carried a bomb load of 1,000 pounds, which terrified the Viets even more when the bomb racks were loaded with Napalm.

Barely had the fighters cleared the town than their pods of Napalm dropped away, straight into the jungle where we believed the Viets to be assembling to attack the town. The Napalm hit the ground with a crashing explosion, sending up jets of flame and heavy clouds of oily, black smoke. The aircraft banked around for a second pass then emptied their machine guns on the Viet positions. Then the ships opened fire, their shells landing unerringly on the same target, directed by a naval fire controller who had joined us when the fire control order was passed on. For fifteen minutes dozens of shells rained down on the small area of jungle, then they ceased fire. Part of the jungle was ablaze. Clearly any of the enemy who were still in that area was dead or dying, roasting even before they got to hell.

We had a brief period of quiet. There was little to be done, we were dug in, all we had to do was wait. Then they came, where the edge of the jungle had been empty it was suddenly filled with men, charging straight for us, their ugly, hate filled faces screaming their battle cries.

"Open fire!" the shout went up all along our line. First the MG42's opened up, their unique ripping sound sending their message of death into the Viet ranks. Then the rest of us opened up, MP40's, rifles. As the Viets reached our first line of barbed wire, the grenade throwers went into action.

We were receiving fire, both from the attackers and from other Viet Minh posted in the jungle, out of sight. Then mortars began.

The first shell hit thirty metres behind us, destroying a peasant hut. The second was only ten metres away and I saw one of my men fall to the shower of fragments.

"Where's that naval man? I want him here right now, we've got a fire mission."

"Here, Sergeant," the anxious face of the naval lieutenant appeared next to me.

"Fire order for your ships, hit the edge of the jungle, we need to stop those mortars and machine guns," I shouted to him above the intense storm of noise and bullets all around us.

"But Sergeant, it's too near to our lines, it's too risky in these..."

"Get those bloody boats firing, Lieutenant," I snarled at him, "or I'll send you out on your own to deal with the mortars."

He ducked down and got on the radio. Using his map, he gave the fire order. Less than a minute later the first shells arrived, shredding the edge of the jungle and creeping towards our position. The oncoming Viet Minh were torn apart by high explosives and mercifully the mortars stopped firing. Either they were hit, or they were moving to a safer position away from the bombardment.

The Viet Minh valued their heavy ordnance, unlike the men, who Giap treated as disposable stores to be consumed in endless numbers in his human wave attacks.

As quickly as it began the battle ended. Including the damage we wreaked in the jungle, we had taken a heavy toll of the enemy. All around the town the French forces, supported by artillery and navy gunfire, were pushing back the attack. We had beaten them back, for now.

Later that day they attacked again, through the night we repulsed constant nuisance attacks, the Viets trying to wear us down with infiltration tactics. The next day they came again, in strength. We pushed back three more major attacks and dozens of minor actions before we judged they'd had enough. By the evening the jungle had gone quiet. The monkeys had gone swinging back into the jungle.

"Sergeant Hoffman," a runner called, "you're needed at

Headquarters."

"What for?" I asked the man. This was unusual. Normally the message would go through Leforge.

"No idea," he said. "They just said they wanted you and so I came to pass on the order."

He turned and left, I went to inform Leforge and then walked over to Headquarters. When I walked in, the divisional intelligence officer, Colonel Joffre who I knew well, was waiting for me.

"Jurgen," he shook hands warmly.

I first came across Colonel Leon Joffre two years before. His attitude towards a former member of the SS was neither warm nor trusting. He'd lost members of his family to SS atrocities in France, notably when his brother was shot as part of a partisan reprisal. However, times had changed. Uncle Joe was no longer the friendly Russian ally. Instead, he was the ugly face behind the vicious communist uprising in Vietnam, and the SS man who once was his enemy now fought on his side, for France. It was very different.

We had exchanged views on several occasions, the natural reserve that French officers felt towards their men set aside, perhaps because of this unconventional war or maybe as I had once been an officer too. We exchanged pleasantries, and then he came quickly to the matter in hand.

"The communists are getting stronger, much stronger. If we don't strike them hard very quickly, I fear that France will lose this war to these ugly little natives. That would be a catastrophe, so soon after the war in Europe."

"I agree, Colonel," I replied. "What did you have in mind,

more troops?"

"Impossible, Paris has already indicated that they're looking to reduce troop levels in Indochina, not increase them. We need another way."

He paused and looked at me.

"Are you looking for suggestions, Colonel? Because if so, I don't have any. Maybe several divisions of Waffen SS would tip the balance," I smiled.

"I don't think the world is ready for that, Jurgen. My department has come up with a plan, one that involves a small group of men infiltrating Viet Minh held Tonkin. What would you say is our greatest problem at the moment?"

I didn't need to think, there was only one name at the top of communist assets that was tipping the war away from France.

"Giap," I told him, "without question. A very clever general and ruthless enough to squander every poor peasant in Indochina to get the communist paradise he's seeking."

"Agreed, I have arrived at exactly the same conclusion. We've decided to recruit a unit to go into Giap's base area," he hesitated. The reason came to me in a flash.

"You want him killed, Colonel. You want me to take a party of my men and apply SS partisan hunter tactics to the problem, yes? A straightforward murder mission."

Joffre looked embarrassed.

"I wouldn't put it quite like that, Jurgen."

"So how would you put it?"

He looked me in the eye.

"You know I can only go so far, say so much. I have French army politics to consider. Let's just say I don't disagree with anything you have just said and leave it at that. What do you think?"

"I am not optimistic, Colonel, it could be a suicide mission. But let me think about it."

The mission was scheduled to depart in four weeks time, after the rainy season had ended and timed to coincide with a French army offensive to the North of Hanoi, which would divert Viet Minh attention from the infiltration mission. Colonel Joffre gave me two weeks to come to a final decision. In the meantime, he allowed me to discuss it with my own NCO's, but not with the men, and definitely not with Leforge.

"The last thing I want is this mission to be tossed around in the officers' mess, Jurgen. You and your trusted NCO's, that's it, no more."

I found Vogelmann, Bauer, von Kessler and Schuster sat outside a bar, relaxing and chatting with a couple of dusky native girls.

"Get rid of them," I said, looking at the girls.

"You don't know where they've been. Besides, we need a private chat."

The women were sent off, they left sulkily. We pulled our chairs closer together and I explained Joffre's mission. There was a shocked silence.

"Giap," Vogelmann said, "will have more protection that the president of France. Do you think we'd ever get near him?"

"Us, no. But Russian military advisors, probably yes."

"Ah," he replied, "so that's it. They want Russian speakers."

"I suspect that's one of the reasons, yes," I told him. "I think the other is that they want people who are not too squeamish about killing."

"Like former SS men, you mean," Bauer smiled.

"Exactly," I grinned at him.

"I suppose we weren't always too fussy in the old days, Jurgen," said Bauer. "We did tend to shoot first and ask questions afterwards."

"Shit on the questions," Vogelmann grinned, "I used to tell my men just to shoot first then move on."

We spent the next hour chatting about possible options for the mission. There were lots of things to look at. It was by no means a simple plan. Getting in would not be too difficult. Getting close to Giap, even with us speaking Russian, which we all did to some degree, would be much more difficult. And after he was killed, getting out, would be a problem on a whole new level.

Giap was their national icon, after Ho Chi Minh. Killing him could stoke up so much opposition that escaping may be an insurmountable problem. My inclination was to say no to Joffre. My men had sacrificed enough. They were in the Legion in Indochina to rebuild their lives and identities, not to throw away what life they had left to them. I felt it was a job for the air force, combined with some good intelligence on the ground about Giap's movements. A squadron of fighter bombers could do the job, blast his headquarters apart and be back at base in time for evening drinks.

Three days later, we were back in action at Phu Ly, south of Hanoi, where the Viet Minh 304th Division had attacked in force.

CHAPTER THREE

Headquarters received an urgent radio message from Phu Ly, the town was under attack. Giap was developing his strategy of wearing down the French forces by mounting large attacks, rather than using clever or subtle tactics. It was a clever move, in theory. He could lose men at a rate that would bring down governments in any civilised country. Ten thousand deaths to knock out a simple French outpost was a price he was happy to pay, at least in terms of his men's lives. The Viet Minh master strategist stayed relatively safe behind his lines in Northern Tonkin, close enough to slip over the border if our forces managed to get too close. Phu Ly was less than a hundred kilometres from Mao Khe, the Legion sent six APC's for us to travel in. My company packed into the vehicles and set off.

We arrived in the town under fire and quickly set up our headquarters in a single storey baker's shop, long abandoned by its owner. It was in the town centre, near the church. Although the communists waged a campaign against the Christian religion in parts of the country they had overrun, this beautiful little church had so far been spared. The Viet Minh were besieging the northern side of the town, machine gun and rifle fire was smashing into buildings and mortar shells landed. Civilians were running everywhere trying to escape the hail of lead and shrapnel sent over as gifts by their Viet Minh fraternal brethren. This was nothing new, many of us from the SS had seen it often on the Eastern Front, and Russians were always ready to sacrifice their own civilians to get a shot at us Germans. Russian General Zhukov explained after the war on the Eastern front.

"If we come to a minefield, our infantry attack exactly as if it were not there. The losses we get from personnel mines we consider only equal to those we would have gotten from machine guns and artillery if the Germans had chosen to defend the area with strong bodies of troops instead of minefields."

He was known to round up civilians to walk over minefields in advance of his troops, so that the soldiers could be spared to fight the enemy. The communists were certainly consistent.

I sent Private Armand up into the church bell tower to snipe at the enemy. Captain Leforge took half of the company and deployed at the east side of the little town, I took the rest of the men and deployed to the west. We had two battalions of colonial infantry in the centre of the town and they were hard pressed to hold off the enemy attacks, which had quietened down since we arrived. The Viet Minh were obviously waiting to see where we deployed before mounting any further assaults on the town. The ground between the jungle and the first of the buildings was already littered with Viet casualties. Inside the town, we had almost thirty wounded lying around on litters, being tended to by medics. Eight body bags were visible, laid out on the ground under a shop canopy. The infantry officers looked wild eyed, obviously they'd been taken by surprise and suffered casualties before they were even able to begin fighting back.

The colonel in charge of the two battalions was Colonel Sartre and I went to speak to him.

"Yes, Sergeant, what is it?" he snapped.

"Foreign Legion, we've just arrived, one company, Sir. My captain has deployed us to the east and west of the town. Could you tell me the situation, enemy strength and positions?"

"If you need information, your captain can ask me, I don't have time for sergeants," he replied haughtily.

I looked pointedly at the casualties lying on the ground, the body bags, then back to him.

"Then perhaps you should make time Colonel, if you want to avoid many more of these body bags."

His eyes widened, astonished at being spoken to in such an insubordinate manner.

"Who are you, Sergeant, what is your name?"

"Senior Sergeant Jurgen Hoffman, Sir, Foreign Legion."

"I thought so," he sneered. "A Nazi."

I boiled over, the Viet Minh were laying siege to the town, his men were draining away in a steady flow of casualties, wounded and dead and the stupid bastard could only think to drag up old arguments.

"No, not a Nazi," I told him, "French Foreign Legion, trying to stop you getting your silly head blown off, Sir!"

I emphasised the Sir, making it as insulting as I dared.

"Now, will you please let me have some idea as to what is going on with the Viet Minh or do I have to beat it out of you?"

His jaw dropped, I could see spittle beginning to ooze out of his mouth. He was terrified, that was obvious, reverting to the familiar safety of military rules and etiquette to try and protect him from enemy bullets. Fortunately, Captain Leforge chose that moment to join us, he saluted the Colonel.

"Sir, we need to know where the enemy is deployed, their strength, anything you can tell us to help get you out of this situation."

He looked from me to the Colonel, curious about the frigid atmosphere. Colonel Sartre hesitated for a moment, and then a mortar shell exploded in the nearby town square, causing him to flinch. He looked wildly around him, and then took the opportunity to pass on his responsibilities.

"Lieutenant, give this officer the intelligence he requires, I'm going to check the stores situation. Carry on."

He hurried away. The infantry lieutenant avoided my eyes, just handing me the maps and radio reports from their positions around the town. It took Leforge and me a few minutes to work out that the situation was grim.

We were under attack from the Viet Minh 304th Division, together with elements of at least two other unidentified Viet Minh divisions. We were faced by possibly several thousand men and our French forces, including the Legion, were little more than a thousand. It looked to us as if Colonel Sartre had almost thrown the battle away before it started, leaving whole sections of the town unguarded for Viet Minh squads to come surging in. Which in fact, they did. Hurling themselves at the defenders in suicidal rushes allowing them to be slaughtered them in droves, but slowly whittling away the numbers and morale of our men. Personally, I would like to have seen Colonel Sartre on the Russian Front, possibly these Viet Minh would give him a flavour of what it was like to be there. I had to laugh inwardly at my vision of a tropical version of the battle of Kharkov.

"Time to go, I think, Sergeant, we've got a battle on our hands, thanks to the good Colonel."

"Yes, Sir, I'll rejoin my men."

"Captain, I could do with some advice on deploying my own men."

It was the lieutenant, standing next to the map table. Leforge looked him up and down, neat and freshly pressed in his new uniform.

"Your first battle, Lieutenant?"

"Yes, Sir, I'm sorry. Lieutenant Mathieu."

"Don't be sorry," Leforge replied. "You've done the right thing, asking advice from someone who's done it before. Do you have a good sergeant, one with plenty of experience?"

"Er, yes Sir, Sergeant Villeneuve, he's been here since the start."

"Good. Go to him, ask his advice and put yourself in his hands. If you're lucky, he'll keep you and your men alive. I suggest you go now."

"Yes, Sir. Thank you Sir."

He hurried off. We looked at each other. Just young lads!

By the time I got to my men on the east of the town, they had deployed, two each of the MG42's stationed at each of our flanks and each gun had several spare belts ready to hand. The men had taken up position behind whatever cover they could find, in the empty windows of the few brick built houses, several behind a concrete statue commemorating some long forgotten hero, some had upturned a pair of vehicles, rusting broken down cars probably left over from the Japanese occupation. They had spare ammunition and grenades ready to hand and everyone was well camouflaged behind some sort of cover.

"Petrov," I called, "did you manage to mine the approach?"

"Sorry, Jurgen, the monkeys have got the open ground covered, I tried to get out there but nearly got my arse shot off for my pains."

"Thanks for trying, anyway."

I checked around our positions. The men were well prepared, there was nothing to do but wait. Occasionally I heard a crack, followed by a scream. Armand was doing his job well, sniping from the church tower.

Then they came. A whole stream of men, the Viet Minh charged out of the jungle, screaming, ferociously. As they emerged, mortars started lobbing shells into the town, throwing clouds of dust, smoke and debris, making it difficult to see what had been hit. Their flanking DP machine guns opened fire with a continuous clattering, spraying rounds around our positions. It was like being in a hailstorm, a very lethal hailstorm. It was not one sided, our troops needed no orders to fire, ignoring the incoming bullets the MG42's opened up at long range. As the Viets got nearer, it was the turn of the submachine guns, not the most accurate of weapons, unless at close quarters. But there were so many attackers that it was literally a case of point and shoot.

I saw dozens of the charging men go down hit by our bullets, but most reached our outer defences, the rolls of barbed wire that the infantry engineers had placed around most obvious approaches to the town. They leapt over the wire, many to be hit by the increasing rate of fire that we brought to bear. In the distance I could hear our troops, the Colonial Infantry and the other half of our company, exchanging a blazing rate of fire with their attackers. Clearly there would be no hope of calling on them to reinforce this position, which was now very hard pressed.

I could see two of our men down, neither moved. At this rate, we were going to take a great many casualties.

I shouted to the men, "Grenades!" and watched them lob the missiles at the Viets. The explosions and rain of metal fragments resulted in more screams, more bodies torn apart and falling to the ground. It was looking grim. I estimated the enemy force was at least five hundred strong. At best they'd lost a hundred men to our gunfire, but that left four hundred to close in on us. There were too many, we couldn't fight those numbers at close quarters.

"Jurgen, get them to pull back, I've planted mines all around our positions," a voice shouted.

It was Petrov, our Ukrainian demolitions expert. I looked around, there were wires snaking back to a house a hundred metres further into the town.

"Yes, that's where the detonator is positioned. As soon as the Viets overrun this position we can blow them back to Moscow."

"Excellent, Nikolai," I told him.

I got out my whistle and blew three short blasts, the signal to fall back. The men looked up, saw me pointing to the position one hundred metres away, and then followed me as I ran towards it. They needed no second order, they literally scooped up their guns and ammunition and were hurtling away from the positions while the Viets were still fifty metres away.

The last man dived under cover just as the Viet Minh surged over our first defence line. I waited for a few moments as they milled around, to let more troops come up to the kill zone. Then they saw Petrov's wires. There was a screech of alarm but it was too late, I turned the switch and the whole area erupted in a massive explosion of smoke and flame. The screaming started, it went on for a long time. At least half of the Viet Minh battalion that had attacked us lay dead or dying. The rest of them were either wounded or too shocked and stunned to respond. There was only one order to give.

"Forward, attack, finish them off. Follow me!"

In a flash, a literal flash, the situation had changed. The surviving Viet Minh still outnumbered us but they were slow, shocked, and unable to think or even defend themselves. We gorged ourselves on killing. The riflemen had fixed bayonets, the rest of us charged in with our MP40's blazing, emptying magazine after magazine into the demoralised troops.

They never had a chance. We killed them in batches, empty

a clip, a line of men dead or dying, reload, another clip empty, another line of corpses. Some of them tried to flee but our MG42's had set up position behind a broken and shattered bungalow, firing from gaps between the broken masonry. They chewed into the retreating troops, flinging them brutally to the ground.

A few, a very brave few, tried to regroup and fight back. We lobbed grenades into the middle of their ranks before they could even take aim, more bodies were flung into the air. Finally, it ended.

Perhaps a hundred of the five hundred who attacked had managed to find the safety of the jungle. We had inflicted a stunning defeat on a much larger force, almost wiped out an entire battalion. That would make them think twice before they hit us again. A shout came towards us from the town. "Sergeant Hoffmann, they need help, quickly!"

I looked up, it was Lieutenant Mathieu, the colonial infantry officer.

"What is the situation, Lieutenant?" I asked.

"The Viet Minh, Sergeant, they've broken through in several places, if we don't stop them they'll come in behind us."

"And Colonel Sartre?"

He hestitated. "I, I, er, cannot find the Colonel."

He looked shamefaced. We both knew what he meant.

"Very well. Bauer!" I shouted.

"Jurgen, what is it?" He came running up to us.

"Friedrich, the colonials have got trouble, the Viets have overrun them in several places. I'm taking some men to give them a hand, keep ten of the men here to watch this area, you can keep two of the MG42's," I told him.

"We need to move fast before the monkeys outflank us."

He dashed away, calling out the names of troops he needed to stay with him. I shouted for the rest of the men to disengage and assemble with me. We'd lost four men killed in the short action and half a dozen wounded, it meant we had around eighty men to help out the infantry. It would have to do.

"Lead the way, Lieutenant, let's move."

"Er, right, you want me, er..."

"Lieutenant, run! Wherever the action is, that's where you're taking us."

"Right."

We followed him, sprinting along. Suddenly we came across a pocket of Viet Minh setting up a machine gun, one of their Russian DPs. They were as surprised to see us as we were to see them, but we were faster, more experienced, more ruthless. Without even checking our speed, our two dozen machine pistols fired into them, three grenades were lobbed over our heads to land in the middle of them. Then we were past, leaving a dead and dying machine gun crew bleeding on the street.

We came to the colonials' position. They were desperately fighting against a much larger force of Viets, obviously another battalion that had launched a separate attack on them. It was not a moment too soon.

"Sergeant Schuster," I shouted to Paul, "keep ten men back as a rearguard, we don't know how many of them have already got past the colonials. The rest of you, come with me, give them everything you've got. Charge!"

We jumped into the battle, the attackers were literally fighting hand to hand in some areas. I noticed the MG42s deploying to our flanks, they would deter any more of the monkeys from getting into the close quarter fighting. Then we hit the body of struggling men. I tripped over the body of an infantryman, righted myself, and then found a snarling Viet in front of me. I fired a burst, saw him go down. Then there was another man behind him. I fired again, he went down. And so it went, but we were turning the tide of battle, the unexpected arrival of our eighty men, seasoned veterans all, bloody fighters, survivors of countless battles, we gave no quarter. The Viets died where they fought, shocked by our ferocity, a ferocity wrought in the course of our long struggle against communists everywhere. These were not men, not even monkeys. Monkeys at least should expect some respect. No, these were inhuman beasts, the denizens of Stalin and Ho's deepest, darkest schemes. They were rats, vermin, to be exterminated. And so we exterminated them, we hacked and slashed at them, shot them. I saw more than one legionnaire strangling his victim to death, the white, blazing heat of barbarous savagery.

We were winning, the Viet Minh couldn't withstand our fresh attack, slowly they began to edge back, and then finally they turned and ran. The men let out a cheer.

"Don't follow," I shouted, "we don't know what they've got waiting in the jungle. Help the wounded, clear the dead and break out the ammunition stores. Let's get this lot cleared. We don't know when they'll be coming back."

They started to carry out my orders. Men were running back and forth, carrying wounded soldiers, a man ran past with a box of machine gun ammunition. Then the sound of a commotion broke my concentration.

"Who the hell authorised the Legion to give orders to my men?"

It was Colonel Sartre, red faced, apoplectic. I looked at him coolly.

"I did."

"You? A sergeant? I will report you for this, consider yourself lucky not be under arrest. I gave orders to these men, I expect them to be obeyed, not ignored because of a Foreign Legion sergeant."

At first he looked satisfied, he'd publicly upbraided this Nazi. Then I laughed in his face and grabbed him by the front of his jacket. I put my face close to his and spoke quietly.

"You stupid, cowardly, jumped up piece of shit."

I could feel him shaking, with both anger and fear.

"You've got men dead here, you turd. Dead because you were too cowardly to come and lead them properly, like an officer. If you don't get reported for cowardice and deserting your men in the face of the enemy, I might even shoot you myself."

I looked around. A group of men, his and mine, were gathered around enjoying the show.

"Now I suggest you either start to act like an officer or get your pistol, put it in your mouth and blow your yellow brains out. Sir!" I shouted.

I felt him flinch, then I flung him to one side and walked off, leaving him white and trembling.

There were a few officers like that in the French army in

Vietnam, although I never encountered anything similar in the Legion. Most officers that I fought with were brave soldiers, even in the face of overwhelming odds and a political situation that seemed to be totally stacked against them. I looked for Lieutenant Mathieu and found him nearby, chatting to Bauer.

"Lieutenant Mathieu, I suggest you start organising your men. I've strong doubts that the good Colonel will be good for very much. Keep an eye out for him, cowards can be very vindictive," I told him.

He nodded, "Thank you, Sergeant, for everything you and your men have done today."

We kept a close eye on the jungle for the rest of that day, but the Viet Minh seemed to have lost heart. We made sure guards were posted and settled in for the evening. Sometime after ten we were sitting around a fire in the square, drinking some of the local rice wine that someone had bought from an opportunistic seller who was making the rounds of the troops, selling his wares. Suddenly we heard shouts from nearby. We hastily picked up our weapons and ran for the source of the trouble. Two shots rang out in quick succession, then a burst of submachine gun fire. We ran around a corner and straight into a hand to hand fight between Viet Minh and eight of our colonial infantry, who had bumped into the Viets as they patrolled the town.

We waded into the melee, picking our targets. One Viet, a wiry, tough fighter, has already killed two of the infantry. I headed for him, he saw me coming and raised his pistol, a Russian Tokarev, a common side arm from the Russian Front. I hit him square in the chest with a burst from my MP40 and saw him spin to the ground, his entrails spilling out. One fighter who wouldn't trouble us again. The others were quickly despatched.

Apparently, they'd hidden in the town, waiting for dark to come out and attack us from behind. They cost us two men, and I immediately gave orders for the town to be turned upside down to find any more Viet Minh who were still in hiding. It was almost two o'clock before we had finished, the men grumbling and moaning that there were no more enemy in the town, it was a fool's errand. But Vogelmann and Kessler had found two more Viets, both slightly wounded and probably waiting for the middle of the night to break out. We sent them to join their other comrades.

We spent all the next day helping the colonial infantry repair the town defences against the possibility of another attack. It was doubtful, the Viet Minh were known to be fight and run soldiers. Long, drawn out campaigns were not unknown, but still uncommon. Two more battalions of infantry arrived in lorries during the late afternoon, together with plenty of supplies and ammunition. We stayed for one more night, enjoying drinks and good food, part of the extra supplies the reinforcements brought with them, before leaving in the morning. We'd been recalled to Hanoi. I watched with Leforge and Bauer as the men loaded our trucks ready to move out. Vogelmann came over to us.

"Does this mean leave, Captain?" he asked.

"It's been awhile since our last break, any chance of taking a few days leave in the city?"

Leforge raised his eyes to the heavens. None of us had

taken any leave for several months, since Giap's new offensives had started. Apart from the odd day grabbed when there was a rare lull in the fighting, there was little opportunity for anything other than fighting. We were outnumbered, and often felt outgunned, something that was confirmed after the war when a unit comparison established that the Viet Minh were more heavily armed than the average French company. Fortunately we were not the average French company, we suffered the burden of extra weapons and ammunition, in order to give us the edge in a firefight.

But overall, the French army in Indochina was fighting for its life and everyone, apart from the politicians and the General Staff, knew it.

Finally our gear was loaded, the troops piled into the lorries and we began driving back to Hanoi, a distance of sixty five kilometres, about forty miles. Halfway there we reached the village of Nhi Khe, until recently a haven of peace in the midst of a war-torn countryside. The villagers gave allegiance to neither France nor Ho Chi Minh. The whole area was a humid, marshy plain, given over entirely to rice paddies. Each morning the villagers came out to tend the rice shoots, while their children were given good elementary schooling in the village hut that served as a school, council chamber and even theatre when some travelling group arrived to stage a traditional Vietnamese play. They travelled to Hanoi and sold their rice to the merchants there, refusing to deal directly with either the French or the Viet Minh. They saw themselves as above the war, neutrals.

Now, smoke poured out of the village. Leforge gave rapid commands, his leading vehicle came to a halt, the rest stopped and we all deployed carefully to either side of the road. If it wasn't an ambush, it was too dangerous to take any chances.

We approached the village warily, but it seemed to be deserted. The huts were in flames, still burning, smoke pouring out. I sent Vogelmann with a small recon section in to check it out. Inside of ten minutes they were back, their faces pale and stretched.

"You need to see this, Jurgen, it's not good," he told me.

"Legion prisoners, they've been..."

He faltered. This was not like Vogelmann, surely he'd seen everything that inhumanity could do to man, in battlefields from the Eastern Front to these steaming jungles. I was wrong.

"They crucified four of them," he told me.

"While they were still alive they cut all over their bodies with knives. Then they smeared what looks like honey on the bodies to attract the local insect life."

I nodded. "We'll move in, we can at least give the poor bastards a decent burial."

I found Captain Leforge and made my report.

"Very well, Jurgen. We may as well take a break here while we get those men buried. Dismount," he shouted to the company.

Men jumped down from the vehicles and advanced warily on the village, weapons at the ready despite Vogelmann's all clear. I heard a shout, it was Senior Sergeant Bauer.

"More bodies, Jurgen, it looks like the villagers."

I went over to where he stood. It was a pit, filled with bodies, men, women and children. Clearly the Viet Minh had tired of the village refusing to ally with them. It looked as if they'd forced them, the men, women and the children, to dig the pit, then made them climb into it and killed them all with rifle fire. The most pitiful sight was of three small children lying on the top of the pile of death, their bodies destroyed by Viet Minh bullets. One child, it looked as if she was a girl, still clutched a wooden doll. I had to walk away, it was too much.

At that time the French had a policy of small forts, often little more than concrete sheds, serving as a defensive line across Tonkin. The theory was that each fort would be part of a network of similar forts, some larger but many similar to the one in this village. When a fort was attacked, the fort could call on a nearby post to send reinforcements. General de Lattre had built up the Vietnamese National Army to provide support for the French, and used these Vietnamese troops to man the so called 'de Lattre Line,' a series of forts and bases. This freed French troops for offensives against the Viet Minh.

So much for theory. What had happened here was repeating itself all across Vietnam, especially here in the North where the Viet Minh were much stronger, both militarily and politically. All the isolated forts achieved was to dilute the French military strength, so that Giap's troops could pick them off one by one. The Viet Minh were anything but stupid. They learned quickly and were utterly ruthless, quick to exploit any French weakness as they had here at Nhi Khe. More French deaths, more Vietnamese deaths. And still they kept building these small outposts. Some said it was the Maginot Line mentality, the fortification built by the French after the First World War to prevent their country being attacked from the east by Germany.

The Maginot Line, named after French Minister of Defense André Maginot, was a line of concrete fortifications, tank obstacles, artillery casemates, machine gun posts, and other defences, which France constructed along its borders with Germany and Italy, in the light of experience from World War I, and in the run-up to World War II.

Belgium was neutral, so the Maginot line didn't extend across Belgium and to La Manche, the English Channel. It didn't need a military genius to work out that to invade France and avoid the Maginot Line, all that was needed was to conquer Belgium, a country with a tiny, weak army. Which, of course, is exactly what the German forces did. Would the French General Staff never learn? Probably not. The problem was that while they refused to heed even the most basic military lessons, soldiers like these poor devils died the most horrible deaths, as did the people they were supposed to protect.

I gave orders to cut down the murdered soldiers, give their tags to Captain Leforge and bury the bodies in a deep grave. There was little we could do for the villagers, they were already in their death pit and beyond our help. Leforge established radio contact with Hanoi, called in a report on the massacre, and then we waited while the burial detail finished the grave. Finally the bodies were buried. We stood in a group around the grave, at attention. Leforge said a few words and six of our riflemen fired a volley into the air. Private Armand, our company sharpshooter played the mournful 'Taps' on the battered bugle he carried around with him in his pack for just such an occasion. Afterwards, we stood for a few minutes in respectful silence. Then we embarked on the vehicles for Hanoi.

"Have you an answer for me, Sergeant Hoffman?" Colonel Joffre asked.

"Colonel, after what we saw today, I would love to hang Giap from a hook on a piece of piano wire," I told him.

"Ah, that's the old Nazi in you, Jurgen, I believe Adolf prescribed that treatment for people he didn't like."

Following the July 1944 attempt to assassinate Adolf Hitler, those suspected of being a part of the plot were brought to trial presided over by the notorious judge of the People's Court Richter Roland Freisler. Hitler said he wanted to see the leaders hung "like slaughtered cattle" and this is precisely what they did at the Plötzensee prison, hanging the condemned conspirators by piano wire or hemp rope from meat hooks. The men endured agonizing strangulation before they died. The deranged Hitler even sent cameramen to film the executions for his enjoyment.

"Maybe," I grinned at him.

"But the answer is no, I'm afraid. Much as Giap deserves to die for encouraging his people to torture and murder innocent civilians, especially the children, I don't believe it is feasible to reach his headquarters, kill him and make an escape. We've discussed it, me and the other NCO's, the consensus is that we would be committing suicide. Sorry."

Joffre showed me out of his office, chatting as we walked outside into the barracks square.

"Sergeant, think about it again, see if there's any way you think it could be done without getting yourselves killed in the process. I could offer you whatever you wanted. Men, equipment, air support, you name it. Just think about it a little more, fair enough?"

"Fair enough," I agreed.

Just then, Manfred von Kessler came running up to us.

"Excuse me, Colonel," he saluted then turned to me. "Jurgen, we're wanted, Phat Diem, a few kilometres north of here, it's under attack. We're to reinforce them immediately, Captain Leforge is assembling the company now. They're sending two companies, B company is coming with us."

"Talk to me when you get back, Sergeant. Remember, anything you want!" Joffre called after me.

I waved an acknowledgment and we doubled towards the vehicle park where our company was already loading onto four trucks. Captain Leforge climbed aboard the leading vehicle, almost immediately it roared away. Paul Schuster was driving, he smiled at me.

"I get the impression I'm driving a fire engine, Jurgen. All we ever seem to do is put out fires that someone else has started."

I thought about his words, he was right. Was I wrong to refuse Joffre, his mission to assassinate Giap, the Viet Minh military architect, Ho Chi Minh's right hand man, the evil guerrilla leader behind so many of the atrocities we'd witnessed in this country? Of course, whatever the merits and demerits of the mission, it would be certainly asking the Legionnaires to attempt a suicide mission.

We roared into Phat Diem, another depressing little village, another French military outpost, another pile of bodies. Unlike Nhi Khe, we found no butchered, crucified bodies of French soldiers, just the bodies of eleven men, the post garrison, all apparently killed by the Viet Minh in a surprise attack.

Bodies of the villagers littered the ground, this time murdered where they stood, men, women and children, for daring to refuse support and sustenance for the Viet Minh. Another communist 'example' to make sure that the next village cooperated. More women and children, together with their men, sacrificed for the teachings of Karl Marx. More soldiers sacrificed by the military geniuses of France on the altar of their South-East Asian Maginot Line.

We had time to bury the soldiers, there were just too many villagers so we stacked them in a heap and left them for locals to attend to. It was the best we could do for the poor devils, the local area was probably still infested with Viet Minh and time for giving a decent burial to all of them was a luxury we just didn't have. Then we mounted the vehicles and returned to Hanoi.

I was very thoughtful. Unlike Phu Ly, these last two villages were beyond fire fighting, we were just acting as a burial detail for the victims. Surely there must be a better way to fight this war than counting our own dead? As we dismounted in the barracks in Hanoi, a soldier ran up to me.

"Colonel Joffre needs to see you, Sergeant, he said to call in as soon as you returned."

I returned his salute and walked over to Joffre's office. When I walked in he wasn't alone. There was another Legion sergeant with him and Joffre's second in command, Major Schumacher, who was a Frenchman, despite the German name. Apparently his father was German, but he was born and brought up in France by his French Parisian mother. I knew Schumacher slightly, a good officer, always ready to lend assistance to any of the men under his command.

"Jurgen, it's good to see you safely back. Major Schumacher you know, this is Sergeant Werner Muller."

We shook hands.

"Muller," Joffre continued, "like you was a member of the Waffen-SS. He was with Otto Skorzeny, a part of the SS-Sonderverband z.b.V. Friedenthal, Skorzeny's own unit.

Otto Skorzeny was an SS-Obersturmbannführer, or Lieu-tenant Colonel, in the Waffen-SS during World War II. After fighting on the Eastern Front, he commanded a rescue mission that freed the deposed Italian dictator Benito Mussolini from captivity. Skorzeny was also the leader of Operation Greif, in which German soldiers were to infiltrate through enemy lines, using their opponents' uniforms and native language. At the end of the war, Skorzeny was part of the Werwolf guerrilla movement.

"That's very interesting, Sir," I replied to Joffre, "but I'm not quite certain what you mean, what are you telling me?"

"I'm telling you, Sergeant, that Muller was one of the team who rescued Mussolini from Gran Sasso, after he was impris-oned by the Allies.

Mussolini was held in the Campo Imperatore Hotel at the top of the Gran Sasso mountain, and only accessible by cable car from the valley below. Skorzeny flew over Gran Sasso and took pictures of the location with a handheld camera. An attack plan was formulated by General Kurt Student and Skorzeny.

On September 12, the Gran Sasso raid was carried out ac-cording to plan. Mussolini was rescued without firing a single shot. Flying out in a Storch airplane, Skorzeny escorted Mussolini to Rome and later to Berlin. The exploit earned Skorzeny fame, promotion to Major and the Knight's Cross of the Iron Cross.

Joffre smiled. "I'm also asking you, Sergeant, asking you, not ordering, to talk to Muller, with a view to mounting a similar mission on Giap."

"You mean kidnap Giap, lift him from under the noses of the Viet Minh High Command?"

"Exactly, Jurgen. That's exactly what I mean, kidnap him, bring him back here, if possible. If not, well, there's the other solution. Talk to Muller, I believe it could be done, without unnecessary risks to the men. Just talk to him. Major Schumacher is here as liaison between you and myself. His job, his only job, is to advise and facilitate on this mission. Talk to Sergeant Muller, introduce him to your NCO's, and then let me know if it can be done. Any questions you have, Major Schumacher will advise. Report to me by noon tomorrow. Dismissed."

We saluted and I left the office with Muller. I was reeling with surprise. I'd been thinking about the problem of how to hit the Viet Minh, for once to take the initiative. Now Joffre had produced this tough looking SS veteran to show us how it could be done. Was this a stroke of fortune, or was it to be chiselled on my gravestone?

I took Muller straight back to our quarters to talk to the NCO's, Bauer, von Kessler, Vogelmann and Schuster. I could imagine their surprise, Skorzeny was one of the real stars of the SS, and anyone who had taken part in the Mussolini rescue would have a good tale to tell.

CHAPTER FOUR

Muller did indeed have a good story to tell. Like many in post-First World War Germany, he remembered the hard times. Born in 1917, his father had been killed during the spring offensive of 1918 when our German forces had spent the last of their strength in a futile effort to break through the Western Front. His mother brought him up in Leipzig, where he remembered the hunger and poverty that followed the Versailles reparations that cruelly reduced an already bankrupt Germany into almost total ruin.

The Treaty of Versailles was signed at the end of World War I. It finally ended the state of war between Germany and the Allied Powers. It took six months of negotiations at the Paris Peace Conference to conclude the peace treaty, and laid the foundations for the Nazis to sweep to power in the shattered state that was Germany following the economic collapse of the 1920's. Germany was obliged to accept sole responsibility for causing the First World War and, under the terms the treaty to disarm, make substantial territorial concessions and pay reparations to certain countries that had formed the Entente Powers. The total cost of these reparations was assessed at 31.4 billion US dollars, many economists estimated it would have taken Germany until 1988 to pay. The result of the treaty was a weak compromise that left none contented, Germany was not pacified or conciliated, nor permanently weakened. This would prove to be a factor leading to later conflicts, notably and directly the Second World War.

Even before the treaty was signed, during the influenza pandemic that swept a war-worn and starving Europe after the war, Muller's two sisters and brother died, leaving him an only child of a single mother.

The 1918 flu pandemic, known as Spanish Flu spread widely across the world. Many victims were healthy young adults, in contrast to most influenza outbreaks which predominantly affected young, elderly or weakened people. The pandemic lasted from March 1918 to June 1920, spreading even to the Arctic and remote Pacific islands. An estimated fifty million people, about three per cent of the world's population died.

In the later 1920's Muller was fascinated by the constant street battles between the right wing groups of former solders, the Frei Korps, the Stalhlhelm, the SA, when they met their communist party opponents.

And of course there was Adolf Hitler, the mesmeric Austrian, saviour of Germany, the one man who could 'save' Germany. His mother idolised the Austrian corporal, and so did Werner Muller. In 1935 he joined the SS-Liebstandarte Adolf Hitler, proudly wearing the uniform of an SS-Schütze. One of his officers in the LAH was Otto Skorzeny. When Skorzeny formed the SS-Sonderverband z.b.V. Friedenthal, Muller followed him. Then came an intensive period of training, during which Muller became a competent parachutist. His final mission was Operation Greif, conceived by Hitler, a false-flag operation led by Waffen-SS commando Otto Skorzeny during the Battle of the Bulge.

Wounded during the battle by bullet wounds to both legs, Muller spent the last few months of the war in a hospital bed outside of Berlin. When the Russians arrived in Berlin Muller managed to escape, following little known trails until he reached Allied lines and eventually the safety of Switzerland.

It was a story familiar to us all. We had all, in one way or another, had to find our own way to escape the Allied plans to revenge themselves on the SS, blaming them for all the bad things that happened during the war. Then, like us, he joined the Foreign Legion, finding himself once more fighting the communists.

We all questioned him extensively on his ideas to kidnap, or kill if necessary, Giap.

"There are several factors you need to consider," Muller told us.

"Firstly, security. Skorzeny's previous missions were plagued by lapses of security. When we took Mussolini the operation was very, very tight indeed. Apart from Hitler, Himmler and Skorzeny, the only people who knew the purpose of the mission were us, the troops who were actually involved in it. Security in this place is a joke. That is your first problem."

We all murmured agreement. Everyone in Indochina

seemed to be either actually or potentially sending information on the French military directly to the Viet Minh.

"Secondly," he continued, "the planning and intelligence needs to be first class, beyond anything I've seen in this place, anyway. What you need is..."

He hesitated to say it, but we knew what he meant. German planners, German intelligence. People with the skills and ruthlessness of the SS, the SD, the Abwehr and German military intelligence.

The French, our masters, seemed to be only good at one thing, which was maintaining the status quo, repeating the mistakes their forbearers had made time and time again.

"Thirdly, you need a crack SS unit to go in there and snatch the bastard, or finish him off."

We all laughed loudly. But it was true. French military methods would not suffice. The hard, ruthless efficiency of the Waffen-SS was needed. We'd been one of the best fighting units the world had ever known, before being frittered away in a series of useless operations that decimated our ranks. But if you asked the SS to do the job, they got it done, or died in the process. Our infantry and panzer units had been the most feared in Europe, for good reason.

"Is that it?" I asked Muller.

He nodded. "That's it really, keep it totally secret, first rate intelligence and planning, then send in the SS. That's about it. Of course, I'll be able to help with plenty of operational detail, but those three things are the most important."

He looked at us with interest.

"Do you intend on doing it?"

"We're considering it, Werner. Men, what do you think," I asked them.

Bauer answered first.

"Jurgen, I'm totally sick of seeing the men whittled down in a series of Viet Minh raids, where all we ever seem to do is go in to repair the damage after the enemy had disappeared into the jungle. Take out Giap and we hit them where it really hurts, right in the balls. If it can be done, I'm for it."

Von Kessler spoke up.

"That's true, Jurgen. Taking out Giap could do some real damage, give them a taste of it."

"Werner," I asked Muller, "strategically, what do you think it would achieve, taking out Giap?"

He thought for a moment.

"Before the Mussolini affair we had an operation planned, Operation Long Jump. It was the codename for a mission to assassinate Stalin, Churchill and Franklin Roosevelt at their 1943 meeting in Tehran for a conference to discuss plans for dividing up Europe after the War ended."

He grinned, "The arrogant bastards knew even then they were going to win."

The Tehran Conference, codenamed Eureka, was the meeting of Joseph Stalin, Franklin D. Roosevelt and Winston Churchill between November 28th and December 1st, 1943, most of which was held at the Soviet Embassy in Tehran, Iran. It was the first major conference amongst the Soviet Union, the United States and the United Kingdom, in which Stalin was present. The central aim of the Tehran conference was to plan the final strategy for the war against Nazi Germany and its allies. The chief discussion was centred on the opening of a second front in Western Europe. It was a major opportunity for Nazi Germany to strike a fatal blow against the leadership of its principal enemies.

"Hitler was keen for us to do it," Muller continued. "Kaltenbrunner was the mission planner. Our intelligence had learned of the timing of the conference in October 1943, after we broke an American Navy code. The Fuhrer chose Otto Skorzeny, with the agreement of Kaltenbrunner, to lead the mission. I recall at the time wondering about that mission. Remember, the Sixth Amy had been thrown to the Russian animals at Stalingrad, and Operation Citadelle, the battle of Kursk, had ripped the guts out of what was left of our forces on the Eastern Front. We had to admit it, the Ivans had got us beaten, no question. The only real issue was when would they arrive on the border of the Reich. None of those three, Stalin, Churchill or Eisenhower, was a military genius, and the Fuhrer had by then managed to show what a cock up he could make of making military decisions, so all of those leaders were expendable. But Giap."

He stopped to think.

"That operation at Cao Bang near the Chinese border, was a masterstroke, he really caught the French with their pants down. Since then he's been attacking our outposts, knocking them down like ninepins. Essentially, he's a whisker away from owning the whole of Indochina north of the Red River. Genius or not, he's a very, very clever leader. It's unlikely they have anyone who could replace him. If we could kidnap or kill him, yes, it could certainly affect the whole course of the war."

He looked at us challengingly. "Will you do it?"

I ignored him.

"Karl-Heinz," I looked at Vogelmann, "what do you think?"

"One thing is for sure," he replied, "if it's going to be done, it will need an SS unit to do it. In Indochina we're the closest thing to an SS unit they're likely to get, so it's us or nobody. And yes, I think it's worth doing. I'm in."

"Ok, that leaves you, Paul," I said to Schuster. "What do you think?"

"Definitely," said the former soldier of SS-Totenkopf, "it'll be like old times, get in, hit them hard, get out."

I laughed at him. "Paul, that's exactly the tactics that Giap himself uses."

"Then perhaps he learned from the SS," he replied, smiling. "But that's the way to do it. Count me in."

"It seems your men are all for it," Muller smiled.

"True, but the final decision will be mine, Werner, and I've got a lot to think about. I'm not convinced it could be done without risking the lives of the whole unit. Could we rely on you for advice and support during the planning and operational stages, start to finish?"

"That's why I'm here," he said, "all the way. I'd go with you, if you decided to go, but I've already been turned down by Joffre for the operation. He wants me on his staff, not rushing off getting 'my stupid Nazi head blown off,' so he said."

"That's fine. Any suggestions on unit strength?"

"I understand you'd be going in as Russian advisors?" I nodded.

"Then a small unit, a maximum of twelve men. You'd want

to be parachuted in, as near to Giap's HQ as possible. That's the first obstacle, to find the bastard."

"And the extraction?" I asked him.

"No mountaintop strips to land a Fieseler Storch and take off again, so you'll need to think of something else."

The Fieseler Fi 156 Storch, or stork, was a small German liaison aircraft built by Fieseler before and during World War II. The Storch could be found on every front throughout the European and North African operations in World War II. It will probably always be most famous for its role in Skorzeny's Operation Eiche, the rescue of deposed Italian dictator Benito Mussolini from the boulder-strewn mountain top near the Gran Sasso, surrounded by Italian troops. Skorzeny dropped with ninety paratroopers onto the peak and quickly captured it, but the problem remained of how to get away. A Focke-Achgelis Fa 223 helicopter was sent, but it broke down en route. Instead, pilot Walter Gerlach flew in a Storch, landed in thirty metres (one hundred feet), took aboard Mussolini and Skorzeny, and took off again in under two hundred and fifty feet, even though the plane was overloaded.

We chatted about the extraction, the most difficult part of the operation. Giap's absence would be noticed immediately. From that moment on we would be hunted down like dogs. We had two choices, immediate extraction, or find somewhere where we could hide until the hunt died down. After a while, it became obvious that immediate extraction was the only answer. Hiding for any length of time in enemy held territory was virtually impossible.

"What about a ventilator?" Bauer asked.

A good question, we had two Hiller UH-12A helicopters, nicknamed ventilators, here in Hanoi.

United Helicopters began producing the Model 360 as the UH-12. In 1949 the UH-12 became the first helicopter to make a transcontinental flight from California to New York. When Hiller upgraded the engine and the rotor blades, the company designated the new model the UH-12A. It was the UH-12A that would be adopted by both the French and United States militaries and the helicopter was used in the Indochina battlefield, as much as its limited numbers would allow.

We could use one of the helicopters to take out Giap. After further discussion we decided our best way out would be east to the sea, the Gulf of Tonkin, where we could be extracted by a warship of the French Navy. All Viet Minh eyes would probably be looking south towards Hanoi, the obvious place for us to retreat to. That should give us the time to make our escape.

We drank heavily that evening, discussing the possibilities of taking the fight to the enemy for a change. I was still very uneasy, this whole area was a literal sieve when it came to security, the least leak and we would be going to our deaths.

Vogelmann and von Kessler, both roaring drunk, got into a huge argument that quickly developed into a fight as to which as the better outfit, SS-Das Reich or SS-Liebstandarte Adolf Hitler. Bauer and I let them swap a few blows, then separated them and dragged them off to their rooms in the barracks dormitory. Then we all shook hands and wished each other good night. I reeled as I climbed the stairs to my own room and got into bed. It had been quite an evening, meeting the veteran of Skorzeny's outfit that rescued Mussolini, capped by far more alcohol than was good for me. As I dropped off to sleep the room seemed to be slowly spinning.

I woke with a start, the barracks shook to the sound of massive explosions. We were under attack, here in Hanoi. What the hell was going on? I threw on trousers, boots and shirt and dashed down the stairs, checking the magazine on my MP40 as I ran. I bumped into Bauer who had been coming to get me.

"We're taking mortar fire Jurgen, the Viets have infiltrated the city and set up a ring of heavy mortars all around us. Captain Leforge is calling out the company to mount up and go and hunt them down."

I acknowledged him and ran on to our vehicle park. It was a chaos of running men, shouts, vehicle horns sounding as drivers fought to clear a way out of the tangle ready to hit the open road as soon as they were loaded with troops.

I found my men directed by Paul Schuster. They were throwing boxes of ammunition and MG42's into the back of a lorry, the engine running.

"We're all ready Jurgen, the Captain wants us to split up. We're to turn right out of the barracks and head south-east to try and find the mortar crew that's operating in that area."

"Let's go," I shouted as I jumped into the front seat. "Hit it Private, let's get out of here before one of those mortar rounds finds us."

Our driver was Armand, the sharpshooter. He nodded at me, then threw it into gear, gunned the engine and dropped the clutch. We roared out of the barracks, I could have sworn we hit the sharp right-hand turn on two wheels. I heard another series of explosions as more mortar rounds hit the area in and around the barracks, then we were on the road, heading to the possible site of one of the crews.

"Armand, take the next left turn, we'll skirt around the side of them."

"But, Sergeant Hoffman, that'll take us at least three kilometres out of our way," he protested.

"And out of the way of any possible ambush they have prepared, Private Armand."

He looked thoughtful, "I see, you think they'll be waiting for us, then?"

"I only know we've done this before, many times. If you were the Viet Minh, wouldn't you set an ambush for the enemy you knew were coming to destroy you?"

"The next left turn it is, Sergeant."

Then the side road was upon us, Armand swung the lorry into the sharp turn and we began skirting around to the east of our objective. The explosions were still hitting the barracks area, we could hear them, though more faintly.

Armand drove like a demon, heading for the source of the mortar fire in our sector. Suddenly, there was the soft 'crump' of a heavy mortar being fired, literally within metres of our position.

"Go, Private, straight for them if you can see them."

He stamped on the accelerator pedal and screeched around the next corner. Suddenly, we were confronted with the enemy, caught like rabbits in the headlights of our vehicle. A group of ten Viet Minh were clustered around the mortar, a 120mm Soviet heavy mortar. They were startled, bringing their weapons to bear on us. I could see a DP light machine gun being hurriedly moved around to point in our direction. The mortar crew were unmoving, they'd been about to reload the mortar but were frozen with indecision, did they need to move their equipment or fire another round?

"Ram them!" I shouted at Armand.

"Hit the machine gun first, then the mortar. Get as many of the Viets as you can. Men," I called to the back of the lorry, "in the next few seconds we're about to pass a Viet Minh mortar crew, send them a calling card as we go past."

Armand spun the wheel and headed straight at the Viet Minh. Two of them managed to get a shot off at us, which went wide. Then the lorry hit, smashing into the machine gun, mangling the gun and the crew beneath the wheels. Expertly he swerved the lorry at the last moment and managed to catch the mortar a glancing blow. It toppled sideways, a scream announced that one of the crew had not managed to jump out of the way quickly enough.

Then we were past, but the misery of the Viet Minh was not over. As we swept past them, twenty legionairres in the back pointed their guns out of the vehicle and opened up with a roar of submachine gun fire. As the lorry continued, I heard the ripping sound of the MG42 which they'd managed to get into action. One man was holding it on the side of the lorry while the gunner swept the Viets with bullets and the crewman fed in the ammunition. Armand finally brought the vehicle to a stop, we all jumped out and ran towards the Viets, weapons ready, but there was no need to continue firing.

All of them had been hit in the mad rush, three mortar men and a machine gun crewman run down by the lorry, the rest by gunfire. One of them was still alive, he was clutching a pistol, which marked him out as some sort of an officer. I lifted his head up, he winced in pain. He'd taken at least one round to the stomach, an agonising wound.

"How many mortars do you have deployed in Hanoi?" I asked him.

Through his agony he managed to snarl at me.

"Enough to kill all of you French dogs," he hissed at me.

"I am not French my monkey friend, but still, I do need to know. How many, quickly, or I will make your agony beyond anything you could dream would be possible?"

He looked at me curiously.

"Not French? Where are you from? Why are you here, fighting the Frenchman's war?"

"Not the Frenchman's war, it is a war against you communist filth. We started it in Russia, this is just the second instalment."

He was obviously educated, he'd picked up the inference immediately.

"So, you are German. You will die here, alongside your French masters."

He tried to summon enough phlegm to spit at me but he was too weak, had lost too much blood.

"Karl-Heinz, see what you can do with him."

Vogelmann stepped forward, "With pleasure, Jurgen."

Although we'd all served in anti-partisan operations, Vogelmann had made it a speciality on the Russian Front, especially when it came to interrogating prisoners. He put out his foot, casually rolled the Viet onto his back, then put the foot on the wound.

"Now, my friend, tell Karl-Heinz what he needs to know and I will take my foot off, maybe even get some medical attention for your wounds."

The only reply was an agonised scream, almost inhuman to the ears. I walked away and left him to it. That was when I saw the bodies. The Viets had set up the mortar on what had almost certainly been the front yard of a brothel. They were noted for their puritanical attitude to loose sex, regarding prostitutes as little more than criminals. Prostitutes who plied their trade with the enemy, with the French, were traitors and collaborators in their eyes. Perhaps the brothel staff had refused to let the Viet Minh station their mortar on their premises, but whatever, they had been killed in the most horrific way.

There was a line of wooden stakes in the ground, probably part of a fence line that formed the boundary of the premises. The owner and staff, eight women and two men, had been impaled on the stakes. Their look of pain-wracked horror was a mute testament to what they must have been forced to suffer. We were not angels, neither in the SS nor in the Legion, but this went beyond the very pits of inhumanity, opening the very doors of hell itself.

I shouted to Vogelmann.

"Karl-Heinz, look there. What the monkeys did to the people who lived here."

He glanced over, even in the dim moonlight I could see him blanche. Then he went to work with a vengeance and the captive's screams filled the night air. After a short time I heard him gasping out to Vogelmann, giving him the details of the operation. Then Karl-Heinz pulled out his pistol, a Luger, which many French troops routinely carried in Indochina.

The Luger was made popular by its use by Germany during World War I. The Pistole Parabellum 1908, known more popularly as the Luger, was a toggle-locked recoil-operated semi-automatic pistol. The design was patented by Georg J. Luger in 1898 and produced by German arms manufacturer Deutsche Waffen und Munitionsfabriken (DWM) since 1900. Although since replaced by the Walther P38, our SS troops had used the shorter barrel Parabellum during the war, when it proved to be effective and reliable on the Easter Front. Many Germans recruited to the Legion carried the Parabellum, perhaps for sentimental reasons, but it was still a useful sidearm.

He put the pistol against the prisoner's head.

"My friend, here is a painkiller to help ease your discomfort."

He smiled at the Viet and pulled the trigger. The man fell back dead, his brains spilling out onto the ground.

"Eleven mortars in all, Jurgen," he shouted.

"I've made a note of their positions. We're looking at about two companies of Viet Minh."

"Right, mount up, let's go, we'll get someone to come back in the day and bury these poor women."

We drove away at speed, heading for the next nearest mortar position. We'd been beaten to it by a squad of French paras who were mopping up the last of the Viet Minh. Without stopping we carried on to the next one. We screeched to a halt alongside the long, high wall of a large villa. Bauer jumped up to look over the wall, sure enough the Viet Minh were there in the open courtyard of the villa, they managed to get a shot off at him before he ducked down.

"About twenty of so of them, Jurgen, they're packing up the mortar to leave by the look of it."

It was a difficult situation. We could take them, go in with all guns blazing. But we would inevitably take casualties. I decided on an alternative strategy, one that we had used successfully once in Russia.

"Mount the MG42 on the cab, Paul," I called to Schuster, "the rest of you, dismount."

They all piled out of the vehicle while Paul fixed the machine gun on the mounts that all our lorries had fitted.

"Armand, back off for about fifty metres, then come back and go through the wall. Paul, hit them with the MG42, the rest of us will be right behind. You'd better take a couple of men with you in the lorry to throw grenades once you're inside the courtyard."

Two legionnaires jumped onto the lorry. Armand reversed back for fifty yards, then I gave him the signal.

We stood to one side guns ready as the vehicle surged forward, accelerating until it smashed through the wall. Immediately, the searing, ripping racket of the MG42 began as Paul Schuster opened fire, the noise punctuated by the explosions of grenades thrown from the back of the lorry. We leapt through the gap in the wall torn by the charging lorry. The Viet Minh were milling around, caught totally unawares by this unexpected attack. At least half of them were down, the rest were running aimlessly from place to place, unsure whether to shoot back, shelter from our guns or just run away. One by one, our shattering automatic fire picked them off and flung their bodies to the ground, torn apart by the incredible rate of fire we poured into them. Then suddenly I shouted for the cease fire. The courtyard was a charnel house, a death pit filled with Viet Minh bodies, smashed equipment and the 120mm mortar, now lying destroyed on its side.

"Check out the villa," I called over to Senior Sergeant Bauer.

"Take three men with you. Be careful, there could be more Viet Minh in there, or even booby traps."

He nodded and raced away. The men were watchful, but the silence that had descended on the courtyard suggested we'd killed them all. Some of the men lit up cigarettes and stood quietly chatting. Bauer came out of the villa, shaking his head.

"It's awful. The owners of the place are in there, at least, what's left of them. The Viets have disembowelled them literally, the parents, four children, the servants, all of them. They're lying in pools of blood, with their guts strewn around like Christmas decorations. Not pretty, I'm afraid."

I nodded. I felt sickened. Once again, the French had been caught unawares by the Viets. The night had gone quiet, clearly we had disposed of all the mortar crews.

But they'd won a victory of sorts, although a pyrrhic victory. They were animals, prepared to sacrifice as many men as was needed in order to propagate the party line, which meant, of course, putting themselves in power.

Communist equality was nothing of the sort, but my God, they were good with words. Very good, so much so that the poor devils believed them. Did the peasants who took up arms and fought for the Viet Minh honestly think that when victory came, if it came, the political elite would ever share the spoils with the rest of the population? If so, they should look to the lessons of the Soviet Union, Stalin's Great Purge and the Siberian Gulags.

The Great Purge was a series of campaigns of political repression and persecution in the Soviet Union orchestrated by Joseph Stalin in 1936 to 1938. It involved a large-scale purge of the Communist Party and Government officials, repression of peasants, Red Army leadership and the persecution of unaffiliated persons. It was characterised by widespread police surveillance, suspicion of saboteurs, imprisonment and executions. Hundreds of thousands of victims were accused of various political crimes (espionage, wrecking, sabotage, anti-Soviet agitation, conspiracies to prepare uprisings and coups) and then executed by shooting, or sent to the Gulag labour camps. Many died at the penal camps due to starvation, disease, exposure and overwork. Other methods of despatching victims were used on an experimental basis. One policeman, for example, gassed people to death in batches in the back of a specially adapted airtight van.

We arrived back at the barracks. Our own company offices and storerooms hadn't been hit, neither had our living quarters. Company C hadn't been so lucky, having sustained a direct hit to the men's sleeping quarters, resulting in about a dozen casualties, some fatal. The medics were carrying the dead and wounded out on stretchers.

I felt angry, a white, hot, blazing anger. Our soldiers should never have been hit in their own barracks. It was sloppy work on behalf of French Army intelligence as well as the garrison who should have been guarding in and around the approaches to Hanoi. But the civilians, the poor devils murdered in the villa, small children butchered in the name of Father Ho Chi Minh and the prostitutes, suffering untold agony and torment through their impalement on fencing stakes, it was too much. It went too far. Yes, our SS units in Russia had behaved at times with appalling brutality. But not this, this was too much.

I recalled one famous occasion when Himmler, head of the SS, had to admonish Romanian troops for their brutality on the Eastern Front. Was it a perversion to have limits to cruelty and brutality? I hadn't an answer for that question, but I did have an answer for the Viet Minh. I went to find Colonel Joffre.

It was dawn by the time I found him leaning against a Willys jeep, smoking. He was alone.

"Sergeant Hoffmann," he greeted me.

"Colonel Joffre." I saluted him.

"I heard about the brothel, it must have been a distressing sight. Terrible, the way those girls suffered. I imagine that's why you're here, the Giap mission?"

"Yes," I replied. "These animals need to be stopped. Giap is our best hope, teach them a lesson. We'll be ready as soon as you wish."

"Excellent, Jurgen. I've been going over the plans for the assault. Our troops will be mounting a prolonged assault on Viet Minh bases to the north west of Hanoi. Giap has his headquarters to the north east, near Cao Bang, so hopefully the assault will divert attention from your movements. The navy has been briefed. They'll be landing your party in two inflat-able boats, launched from a destroyer currently patrolling the

Gulf of Tonkin. The air force has made two helicopters available to lift Giap back to Hanoi, and the navy will be waiting to bring you off of the beach when the job is done. If you run into trouble the navy also has the carrier Arromanches waiting offshore, with two squadrons of F6F Hellcats permanently ready to offer assistance. That's about it, a formidable force to support your group, Jurgen."

I whistled, "Indeed it is Colonel, you must want Giap very badly."

"We do, yes, the High Command has given your mission the highest possible priority."

"And if we cannot get him out alive?"

Joffre hesitated. "That's in your hands, Jurgen. Giap is the man behind the crucifixions, the impaling. Are you prepared to leave that monster loose in Vietnam?"

"No," I replied quietly. "I am not."

"Very well. We're understood. You have more than three weeks before the mission begins, use it to thoroughly acquaint your men with every aspect of the mission. I will have the orders sent to you later today. You'll also have every map and piece of intelligence we have delivered to you with the orders. Take a look at it and report back to me by the end of the day. And Jurgen," he added.

"Sir?"

"I want you and your men confined to the barracks until you leave for the mission."

I started to protest, but he held up his hand.

"Jurgen, it's no good. That comes from the very highest authority."

"You mean General de Lattre?" I asked him.

"I mean the President, Vincent Auriol, President of France. He's taken a personal interest in this affair, and it is at his insistence that security must be totally watertight."

"Yes, Sir." We exchanged salutes and I left to tell the men.

The news was an instant success and they let out a great cheer. At last we were being let loose to do what we did best. A hard hitting strike force, partisan hunters, elite troops to hit the enemy where they least expected it. Those were our roles in the SS and that was our new assignment.

The news about being confined to base didn't go down so well.

"You cannot be serious," Karl-Heinz said incredulously.

"I'm afraid so. Orders from the top, the very top!"

We'd been fighting the Viet Minh incursion all night. I had a drink with the men, while we were swapping our stories of the night's activities, the messenger brought in a despatch. I opened the slip and read through it. The men watched me intently as I looked up.

"They're sending us all the maps and reports we need later this morning. We'll assemble here at two after we've had some lunch. We can make final decisions about the mission and choices on the men we'll take with us. A maximum of twelve, so think carefully. They're all good men, but we'll want the best of the best, the experts. I'll see you all later."

As I left the canteen, I noticed Mai St Martin and Thien van Hoc sat at a side table talking animatedly. Vogelmann's and von Kessler's girlfriends. I cursed for not noticing them before, they should not have been present while we were talking about our future mission. I resolved to speak to the two men later.

I left them enjoying a celebratory drink, found my bed and within minutes was asleep. By half midday I was being shaken awake by a corporal from Intelligence, with a satchel of maps and debriefing reports. I reluctantly got up and dressed, then spread everything out on the floor and checked the maps. It could be done, yes, but even with the massive support we were being given, it was still a huge risk. We'd all taken risks before though, we hadn't signed on in the SS or the Legion to carry out desk jobs. Taking risks was our trade. I knew however that this was more than just a risk. It was striking a blow against the very foundations of a rebel government, itself supported by the huge resources of both China and Russia.

We could do it, if all went well. But that was the burning question. If!

CHAPTER FIVE

We spent the following week preparing for the mission. Each day, I took the men out into the jungle for hours of hard, physical endurance training. Petrov managed to blow up several ancient trees, bringing down what had taken probably five hundred years to grow in just a few seconds, but it was good practice for the real thing. Armand set up a variety of targets and practised his sharpshooting, accurately putting round after round into the bull's eye. I made the others run fully laden, along the jungle trails, forcing the pace until they literally fell over gasping for breath. In the evenings our muscles reminding us of the agony we'd gone through that day. We pored over maps and plans of the operational area, fine tuning every detail of the mission until we could recite it in our sleep.

Finally, we were ready to go. I had stuck to the idea of a twelve man unit, enough to hit hard but not so many as to invite discovery by the Viets. Seven of us were former Waffen-SS. That was no coincidence, the experience of the Eastern Front had been won in blood, no amount of training could substitute for the real hell of those dark times. To survive the Eastern Front you had to become a unique survivor, staying alive in the midst of fierce firefights against overwhelming odds, when you were under attack from thousands of savage Russians anxious to wipe out every German from the face of the earth. You had to possess a rare mix of skills. Those were the kind of skills we would need to come back from this mission alive.

Apart from the former SS men, we had Private Armand, perhaps the most skilled sniper I'd ever encountered, and I had encountered many on the Eastern Front where the Russians made sniping almost a national pastime. Sergeant Petrov, the Ukrainian, was our unit demolitions expert. We also had with us Corporal Bruno Dubois, which was most definitely not his real name. He was a muslim from Casablanca who had used his knife once too many times on business rivals in his native country. Probably as a result of his numerous smuggling operations he was an expert with almost every weapon we possessed in the Legion armoury, as well as being a nasty fighter. There were also two other Arabs, Algerians, Privates Laurent and Renaud. Like Corporal Dubois, they were both vicious killers.

I felt as confident as I could be that we were going into this operation with the best possible chance of getting back out. None of my unit was French, a deliberate decision, I had no place for men who might hesitate for a second whilst considering French sensibilities. That also meant no officers, for all our officers were of course French. That suited me fine. I needed brutal killers, not latter day Napoleons.

Before we began, the mission almost ended. Our high command in Paris had received orders from the Americans, who seemed to know every move the French made in Indochina almost before it happened. For whatever reason, they expressly forbade the French Navy to carry troops bound on an assassination mission. Apparently that kind of operation fell 'outside of the US constitution'. The Americans were supplying us with large quantities of logistical support, everything from infantry rifles to fighter aircraft. In return they tapped into virtually all of the intelligence from our civilian and military agencies, building a future store of information for use in their own projected anti-communist operations.

Normally it caused us few problems, but the Americans could be notoriously sensitive where certain matters were concerned. Our operation fell into this category. I suspected at the time that their policy was more of a 'clean hands' policy than any real difference of opinion. After all, they'd forbidden our unit being transported in French warships in the Gulf of Tonkin. There was no mention of other means of transport.

I spoke to Colonel Joffre about the problem.

"The thing is, Sergeant Hoffman, we have to be very careful now that the Americans are aware of what we're doing. Frankly, General Lattre is considering calling the whole thing off."

"That would be a shame, Sir, just because of a minor difficulty with transportation."

He smiled. "The problems are anything but minor, I'm afraid. I sometimes think that politics will be the end of us here in Vietnam. Do you have any suggestions? An air drop, perhaps?"

"No, Sir," I replied.

"Too noisy, too many chances of things going wrong. We need to travel overland, avoiding the main routes. If necessary we'll walk all the way."

"I see," Joffre said thoughtfully. "You really want to do this, Jurgen, you want to nail that bastard Giap."

"I've got nothing against him personally, Sir," I told him.

"But I honestly believe we need to hit the enemy hard, where it hurts. Carry the fight to them. It could shorten the war, and certainly save a lot of French lives. Giap is their main military planner. Some say he's a genius, I'm not too sure about that, but if we kill him they could well think seriously about prolonging the war."

"I agree, supposing we mount a search and destroy mission to the north west of Hanoi? At some stage your unit drops off and goes in a different direction? How would that be? Nothing on paper, of course."

We both smiled.

As we loaded, I noticed Mai St Martin and Thien van Hoc watching again. They saw me look at them, Mai spoke quickly to Thien and they walked away. I'd still not mentioned my worries about them to the men, it would have to wait, it was too late now. When we got back, if we got back, I decided to talk it over with Joffre, we needed a serious look into the backgrounds of those ladies. Then I put it out of my mind as we left our Hanoi barracks, part of a larger, battalion strength column.

A total of six hundred and fifty men, the whole of the Second Battalion, 13th Half Brigade packed into a long line of trucks heading north west, the opposite direction from Cao Bang which lay to the north east near the Chinese border. Ten kilometres out from Hanoi one lorry at the back of the column abruptly left the main highway and began to head north east. We were on the way!

Our first destination was Thai Nguyen, from where we intended to abandon the vehicle and head out along a series of little known game trails, pointing in the direction of Cao Bang. Like most of the north east of Indochina this area was in Viet Minh hands. We were very alert to the possibility of enemy ambush. The Viets tended to come out at night, avoiding the daylight as much as possible with the risk of French air strikes. Our plan was to travel the hundred kilometres to Thai Nguyen during daylight and as fast as possible. Several kilometres before the town we would abandon the lorry and move into the jungle. Corporal Dubois was driving, his foot pressed hard on the accelerator pedal as if he was reliving his old smuggling days in the back streets of Casablanca.

Speed was necessary, this journey carried a high risk and the faster he drove the harder our vehicle would be to hit. Every man was watching carefully through the canvas canopy of the lorry. We were thirty kilometres from Thai Nguyen when we hit the first trouble.

We rounded a bend and came upon a group of twelve Viet Minh clustered around an upturned cart. The cart was pulled by bullocks, the two animals had been released and were grazing quietly at the side of the road. Ten of the Viets were unloading crates from the cart, two more, presumably their officers, were standing nearby. They turned as we swept into sight, astonished at the presence of a French military lorry this far into communist held territory. We had only one chance and that was to eliminate them immediately. If only one escaped they would begin hunting for us, which could end any chance of our mission succeeding. I had no need to give orders, the ten troopers travelling in the back opened fire with an assortment of weapons. Kessler had brought along an old British Bren gun, I heard the stutter of its short bursts first. Then I heard the rest of the unit's weapons begin firing. It was an amazing assortment of ordnance. Bauer, Schuster and Vogelmann had their Soviet made PPSh's, Corporal Dubois had an American Thompson gun, making him look like the gangster he had once been. The rest had infantry rifles, the most effective of which was Armand's, each crack almost certainly finding its target. A Viet officer did his best to unsnap a grenade from his belt, but before he could even pull the pin to throw it at us Armand hit him squarely in the chest, sending him spinning to the dust.

We were lucky that time, within less than a minute the dozen Viets were all down, not one had managed to get a shot off. We dismounted and searched the area. There were no more enemy troops to be found and no evidence that there had been any others to escape and sound the alarm. I heard a shout from one of the men, it was Dubois. He was crouched near to the enemy corpses.

"Sergeant, this one's alive. He doesn't look like a Viet to me."

I hurried over. The man had taken at least two bullets to the stomach. He was bleeding badly, his face screwed up in pain. He was babbling, but not in French, or anything that resembled one of the local dialects. But it sounded familiar.

"Have you checked his papers, Corporal?"

"Yes, Sir, every pocket. No documents, nothing."

I smiled, true to his Arab roots, Bruno Dubois would not fail to check an enemy corpse for loot. Well, they wouldn't need it anymore, so why not? Petrov wandered up, looked dispassionately at the wounded man who was obviously dying.

"He's speaking Chinese, Jurgen."

"Chinese! Are you sure?"

"Definitely. It's a mangled dialect, but I'm certain. He looks Chinese. One of the advisors that Mao is sending over to Indochina these days."

"Shit."

This mission had been hampered by politics even before it got off of the ground. First the American refusal to allow the Navy to transport us and now we had a Chinese national fallen victim to our gunfire. The implications were not good. Even though he was helping our enemy there were no overt, declared hostilities with China. The Chinese victim of a Foreign Legion shooting would hand the communist press a real propaganda victory.

"Petrov, I want him to disappear," I said to the Ukrainian. He smiled.

"Into little pieces, Jurgen?"

"Exactly."

"I shall turn him into mouse droppings. That should make identification a problem for his Chinese friends."

Petrov began to drag the body away into the trees. Ten minutes later he strolled out nonchalantly and we heard a loud explosion. It was time to move. The Viets would most likely assume that their Chinese advisor had been taken prisoner. They could ask for him back and Hanoi would say quite honestly that they hadn't a clue what they were talking about. It was time to move on. We boarded the lorry and Dubois revved the engine, put it into gear and let out the clutch, sending us surging forward. We were more alert than ever, clearly the Viets thought they could freely move around in this area, there could well be more of them along this road.

We met no more Viets before we stopped ten kilometres out from Thai Nguyen. It was as close to the enemy held town as we dared to go. After we climbed down and unloaded our supplies, Dubois drove the vehicle hard into a dense area of jungle. Four of the troopers followed it in and hacked down foliage and vines, weaving them around the lorry which was barely visible anyway. By the time they'd finished it was impossible to see where it had driven in. With any luck, it would be several weeks or even months before it was discovered. Petrov clambered through the foliage with his pack of charges, when he came back he reported to me.

"The next Viet that goes near that lorry will be the last, Jurgen. I've packed enough explosives to blow them to kingdom come and destroy the engine and gearbox at the same time. It's all connected to trip wires, so if anyone has left anything behind it would be best if they forgot about it."

"Well done, Nikolai. Ok, men, lets move out," I shouted.

We marched into the dense jungle, following a tiny game trail that was marked on one of our old maps. I was slightly worried, it was not as overgrown as it should have been, so I made certain we had two men at the point and two bringing up our rear, just in case. We made good time, within three hours we had covered almost ten kilometres. Then we came upon the village.

Our point men Armand and Renaud came running back down the path.

"It's a small village, Sergeant, about ten or twelve huts, maybe one and a half kilometres up the path. It looks as if it's been taken over by a small Viet Minh unit, we can see eight of them altogether."

"What state are they in? Do you think they heard us?"

"No, they're sitting around listening to one of their people giving a speech, a commissar or an officer probably. No sign of any lookouts, they're probably not expecting any enemy in such a remote part of the country."

"Very well, go back and keep an eye on them, but stay undercover. We'll have to take them, there's no other way past this village that I can see. It could take us days to cut through the jungle."

They jogged back up the path while I gathered the men around me. I described the way we would attack the village.

"The most important thing to remember is that our mission takes priority. That means that no one is to escape and alert the enemy that we're coming. The scrap we had back on the road will be written off to a mobile patrol, or even and air attack. But this is different because the trail leads in only one direction."

I sent the machine gun crews to get in position on each flank of the village. The rest of us prepared with our submachine guns and grenades, we dumped our heavy packs behind a tree and moved off.

The Viet officer was still talking, screaming would better describe his technique. Whether he was admonishing them for some failure, or whipping them up into a fury to go and fight the enemy I couldn't be sure. Neither did I care. I was here to kill him, not to listen to him. I looked around. Armand had climbed a tree and was waiting patiently with his rifle. I couldn't see Renaud, but assumed he was similarly ready. Schuster told me that the machine gun crews had reported in ready. I waited for a few minutes, but no other Viets showed themselves, neither were there any civilians in sight. It was not unusual for the communists to kill all the villagers if they didn't get instant obedience when they took over.

I took a final look around then cocked my submachine gun, a German MP38. I took aim at the group of men, they were too far away for precision shooting, selected 'auto' with the selector then held the trigger down. Almost before the first couple of bullets had left the barrel the others opened up. Within seconds hundred of rounds hammered into the enemy group, knocking them down into bloody ruin before they even realised what had hit them. This was the form of warfare we had practised so many times on the Eastern Front, where we learned to never let an enemy escape to start shooting back at you from behind cover. Like the French here in Indochina we were heavily outnumbered in Russia, we simply had to kill the enemy in large numbers before they could overwhelm us with their superior numbers and ordnance. The MG 42s buzzed from the flanks, Armand and Renault fired shot after shot into the group. In less than a minute I shouted to cease fire. With our ears ringing, we walked carefully into the village to check the bodies. They were all dead, eight more sacrifices to the glory of Father Ho.

"Sergeant Bauer, check the surrounding area, make sure they're all accounted for."

"Will do, Jurgen. A good shoot, I think."

I nodded at him. A good shoot indeed. Von Kessler and Schuster were already rifling through their packs for signs of any documents we could keep for Headquarters to look at. The Arabs, Dubois, Renaud and Laurent, were rifling the possessions of the dead Viets, continuing a tradition of looting the fallen that they'd probably learned at their grandfather's knee.

Bauer walked out of the jungle, with an astonishing sight, a woman. A beautiful, though grimy and shabbily attired white woman. He also had a couple of dozen other civilians with him who looked to be Viets.

"What the hell is that?" I asked him.

"These are the survivors from the village, Jurgen. The Viets kept them locked in a compound a couple of hundred metres down the path. Apparently used them as servants and porters."

"And the white woman?"

"I can speak for myself, Sergeant, I do speak French," she cut in.

I looked at her. She was about five feet tall, which made her no bigger than the Viet natives who tended to be short in stature. She was very slim, yet the dirty ragged clothes she wore failed to hide her curvy figure. Her dark brown hair was cut short, as was the custom in Indochina for European women, long hair was difficult to keep clean and tidy. Her eyes, dark brown, looked at me without a trace of diffidence.

"What's your story, mademoiselle?" I asked her.

"My name is Helene Baptiste, Sergeant. I'm a doctor. I work for the French government carrying out a survey of the diet of the natives in selected parts of Indochina. I was working here when the guerrillas came, they killed most of the men and took the rest of us prisoner."

"How long have you been here?" I asked her.

"I think about eight months. It's difficult to keep track, we have no clocks or calendars."

It was hard to imagine the suffering of a white woman in this Viet hell. They were hard enough on their own people, I didn't like to ask how bad it had been for her. I looked around, four of the men were standing guard, the rest were helping to tend to the natives, who were in a bad way after spending so long at the tender mercies of the communists.

"We've limited medical supplies but you are welcome to use some of them to take care of the villagers. They look as if they need them, are you in need of medical attention or can you give my men a hand?"

"I'm a doctor, Sergeant, I will help out as much as I am able. And no, I'm not in need of anything urgent, apart from a shower and some clean clothes, that is."

She smiled, a smile that seemed to brighten up this dull, decrepit native village.

"Very well, I'll leave you to it."

"Thank you, Sergeant, for rescuing us. What is your name, I cannot call you Sergeant?"

"Jurgen."

"Please call me Helene."

She smiled again, my God, she was beautiful. I made a note to warn the other sergeants to watch out for her, any of the men would have given a year's pay to spend the night with a woman like this.

As I walked away, I wondered what the hell to do with her. I could hardly leave her here, she had suffered enough. Besides, this was Viet Minh territory. They'd be back, sooner or later, this time thirsting for revenge for the deaths of their comrades. When they turned up this village had better be empty, the reprisals heaped upon the heads of anyone still here would be beyond contemplation. The villagers could simply melt into the jungle, this was after all their territory before the Viet Minh came. But Helene could not, a white woman would soon become known to the communists who would come searching for her. I could radio for a helicopter evacuation, but the noise would bring in every Viet Minh fighter within a hundred square kilometres, sounding the death knell of our mission. I could hardly spare any men to escort her back to Hanoi, that left only one option, an option I was loathe to take. She would come with us, after all she was a trained medic.

I called my sergeants, Bauer, Schuster and Petrov to one side, we all lit cigarettes while I quietly explained it all to them.

"Damn, Jurgen, that's a great idea. A beautiful doctor along with us, what more could we ask for?" Petrov exclaimed.

"It's not ideal, Nikolai, she could hold us up. She's a doctor, not a soldier. But I simply can't see any alternative."

"True, Jurgen," Bauer nodded thoughtfully.

"But if that's the only option open to us, we'll need to make the best of it. She's survived this long in a Viet Minh hell hole, she's probably a lot tougher than she looks."

"I thought you were Frenchmen," a voice said behind me.

It was Helene, who had come up quietly to our little group. We'd been speaking in German, as we often did by habit in this French speaking country, it gave us a small degree of anonymity.

"France is our adopted country, Helene," I replied. "We were speaking German, did you understand what we were saying?"

"No, I don't speak German. So are you all Germans?"

"Before we joined the Legion, yes, except for Nikolai, who is Ukrainian," I replied in French.

"So you fought in the war. Were you Nazis?"

"We were Waffen-SS. After the war we joined the Legion and took French citizenship."

"SS, I see, so you were Nazis."

"It's complicated," I replied.

"Helene, we were soldiers, we fought for our country just like Frenchmen, Americans and Englishmen. There was no difference."

"Except for the atrocities you committed, millions killed, the Jews, gassed, exterminated."

Her eyes were fiery, I wondered what she'd suffered at the hands of the Germans during World War II. I didn't have to wonder for long.

"Both of my parents were killed by the Nazis, Sergeant, for me they were a gang of brutes and thugs."

"I'm sorry for that, Helene, but I assure you I have never attacked anyone who wasn't carrying a gun and ready to shoot at me. Isn't it ironic that you have been rescued by the very Germans that you hate so much?"

She stared at me, then abruptly stormed off. We could debate the rights and wrongs of war endlessly, but we were here to do a job. Hers was to heal the sick, mine was to kill the enemy. Soldiering was a job like any other, there were good soldiers and there were bad soldiers, as there were good and bad doctors.

I carried on with my job, organising and checking supplies and munitions, making sure the sentries were alert. I came across Helene, she was sat on a tree stump, weeping.

"I'm sorry for being so rude, Jurgen," she murmured.

"You're right, of course you didn't kill my parents, I was wrong to blame you. War has been unkind to me, both the war in Europe and now this one in Indochina."

"War is an unkind business, I'm afraid. Soldiers just go where they're ordered, if you don't like the war, you must take it up with the politicians. Now, we need to discuss what we can do with you."

"Can you not get me back to Hanoi?"

I explained that we were on a high level, secret mission, that I couldn't spare men to escort her or alert the enemy by calling in a helicopter evacuation.

"So, I'm offering you a job, cherie, as unit medic. You can come with us and we'll see you safely back to Hanoi afterwards. Or you could stay here, but the Viet Minh will of course return."

She thought for a moment.

"This mission, is it dangerous?"

"We're fighting the Viet Minh, Helene, you have seen it here for yourself. Yes, it'll be dangerous."

"Very well, I understand, Sergeant Hoffman, I will come with you in my capacity as a doctor, nothing more."

She looked me in the eye, then abruptly turned to the villagers and began helping my men tend to their wounds and injuries. Most of them were covered in sores as a result of untreated cuts and grazes, together with the effects of the poor diet. We could help them, but the Viet Minh would return, then God help them if they were still in the area.

Eventually we resumed our march. Armand and Renaud took the point as usual, Sergeant Schuster and Private Fassbinder covered our rear. I was pleasantly surprised that Helene Baptiste kept up, clearly her imprisonment had not affected her too badly. I afterwards discovered she'd been a successful sportswoman in France, a keen skier, tennis player, marksman and at one time a middle distance athlete, narrowly missing selection for the Olympic Games.

She walked beside me and chatted about her life. Born in Lyon in 1924, her parents had moved to Paris shortly afterwards. At school when the Germans invaded, she had returned home one day to discover her parents had been imprisoned and shot by the Gestapo after her father, also a doctor, treated a wounded resistance fighter and was executed together with his wife. Helene had decided that all Germans were the lowest form of life, and dedicated her life to becoming the kind of daughter her parents would have wanted her to be. She graduated from medical school and immediately volunteered to serve in war-torn areas where she felt her talents would be most needed. She was twenty eight years old, and had worked in a variety of places, including Algeria and even a brief visit to Devil's Island, the notorious French penal colony. Eventually she wound up in Indochina, touring remote villages to assess the health problems that needed to be addressed by the government. She'd travelled with a native guide, who'd been promptly killed for collaborating when the Viet Minh arrived in the village.

Eventually, dusk fell over the jungle and we made camp in a clearing. A stream bubbled nearby and we thankfully refilled all our water bottles with the cool, clear water. We shared out our rations and sat contentedly chatting and smoking after we'd eaten.

"Tell me about yourself, Jurgen," she said suddenly. "I've given you my life history, how did you end up in Indochina?"

The others laughed, von Kessler said "Yes, go on, Jurgen, tell the young lady how a Waffen-SS killer wound up in this stinking hell."

"Shut up, Manfred," I replied.

"It's not a pretty story, I can't think anyone would want to hear it."

"I want to hear it," she said. "Please, tell me what brought you here."

I thought for a moment. Then I told her of the riots in Berlin, following Germany's collapse in 1918. The endless violence, rocks thrown, shots fired. The Stalhlhelm, The SA, The Freikorps, mainly right wing civilian irregulars recruited from former soldiers, fighting the rising tide of communism that threatened the whole country. Many of my friends and family members were caught up in the violence. Two cousins had been executed by the communists when Munich was briefly declared a Soviet Republic. The depression, the chronic inflation that wiped out peoples saving, the hunger and desperation that all seemed to be answered by the miracle of Adolf Hitler.

Hitler rose to high office in 1923 mainly as a result of his considerable skills in oratory, organization and promotion. He was aided in part by his willingness to use violence in advancing his political objectives and to recruit party members who were willing to be equally violent, or more so. The Beer Hall putsch in 1923 and the release of his book Mein Kampf introduced Hitler to a wider audience.

In the mid-twenties, the party engaged in electoral battles in which Hitler increasingly participated as a speaker and organizer, as well as in street battles and violence between the Communists and the Nazi's Stormtroopers, the SA. Through the late 1920s and early 1930s, the Nazis gathered enough electoral support to become the largest political party in the Reichstag, and Hitler's blend of political acuity, deceptiveness and cunning converted the party's non-majority but popular status into effective governing power in the failing Weimar Republic of 1933. The Russian front finally put an end to Hitler's ambitions as the German people realised too late that he had let them to utter defeat and catastrophy.

I had joined the Waffen-SS and fought most of the war on the Russian Front, fighting the communists. When the war ended, I'd risen to the rank of Sturmbannfuhrer, or Major. I returned home to find myself a hunted criminal, after so many years of serving my country as a loyal soldier.

Losing the war and the subsequent treatment of the Waffen-SS had left most of us embittered, poverty stricken, jobless and homeless. It was just a short step to joining the Foreign Legion, where I quickly found myself, like many other former members of the SS, once again fighting the communists. It was a different country, a different climate, a different foe. But the rhetoric was the same, the cruelty no different, the fighting no less bloodthirsty.

"But surely, Jurgen, the Waffen-SS was no less cruel in the countries it occupied, especially Russia," she commented.

"Helene, I cannot answer for the Gestapo, or the SS-Ein-satzgruppen that hunted down and murdered Jews on the Eastern Front. They disgusted me and most of my comrades, just as much as they did you and the rest of the civilised world. But we were soldiers, and we fought against enemy soldiers. The communists will kill anyone who disagrees with them, you have seen their methods in that village."

"It is so confusing," she said.

"After my parents were killed, I hated all Germans, I couldn't bear to be near them. If I knew who'd killed them, I would have shot them myself. But now, here I am rescued and being helped by those self same Germans."

"Not the same, Helene, by no means. As I said, we despised the excesses of cruelty carried out in the name of Germany. Those brutes were the exception, not the rule. That's the difference between us and the communists. Cruelty is their 'modus operandi', the very foundation of their philosophy. You either agree with them, or they kill you, as you have witnessed."

Bauer came and joined our little group. He handed out cigarettes then topped up our mugs of coffee with a flask of schnapps he'd taken out of his pack.

"I was in France, training the SS-Freiwillegen units, French volunteers. They were keen, those lads. Sometimes I thought they were too keen, they seemed to be trying to outdo the German SS units by displaying more bravery under fire. More cruelty, too. Did you ever see the Milice units, Miss Baptiste? French paramilitary police? Nasty bunch."

Helene nodded. "I understand the point you're making, Sergeant. That it's not just Germans who are cruel, the French can be just as bad."

"No," Bauer shook his head, "not at all. I think that humankind is capable of the most extreme acts of cruelty, it's nothing to do with nationality. It's more to do with politics, with beliefs. We found that out in Russia the home of communism. They would kill anyone there, soldier or civilian, man, woman or child, just for the crime of not agreeing with them. It's a bit like religion really, like the Medieval Inquisition. One day we'll get another religion go just as crazy, just as bloodthirsty. Maybe they can fight the communists, they could kill each other, save us the trouble."

"Enough of the philosophy," I called, "we need to make an early start, let's turn in."

The meeting broke up, I checked the sentries and set a watch rota. Then I climbed under a blanket and went to sleep. Helene Baptiste was in the middle of us, I had loaned her my bedroll which occasioned a stream of taunts from the men.

In the morning we refilled our water bottles from the stream, it could be the last chance for some time. Then we set off, as before Armand and Renaud took the point, Schuster and Fassbinder were the rearguard. We left at seven o'clock and walked all morning. By midday I was ready to call a halt for lunch when we found ourselves on a well kept trail. It had recently been widened and was obviously well used. The men needed no orders, everyone cocked their weapon and held it ready for instant action.

We scanned the surrounding trees and foliage, but there was no sign of any enemy ambush. Then we walked out of the jungle into an amazing sight, rows and rows of neatly planted rubber trees either side of an avenue that stretched way in the distance to a house. No ordinary house, it was more of a mansion, built in classic French style. As we got nearer I could see that it was not as imposing close up as it had been from a distance. Much of it was in need of repair, but it was still a startling contrast to the mean little huts that the natives built in these rural areas.

Plantation workers were tapping the trees, we saw five of them as we marched up to the house. They were all young men, probably between eighteen and thirty, which was enough to make us even more vigilant. At that age, in this part of Indochina controlled by the communists, that invariably meant Viet Minh. I looked at Bauer, he nodded. He'd come to the same conclusion.

We reached the house and halted, he detailed Renaud and Armand to take post somewhere they could keep watch. The two men disappeared with their rifles, I last saw them climbing a couple of high trees. The front door opened and a man walked out, he was dressed in a soiled white linen suit.

"Gentlemen, this is a surprise. Welcome to my home, please join me for some refreshments."

CHAPTER SIX

I was so surprised that I didn't reply for a few moments. The man was white, probably about fifty years old, and his accent indicated he was French. Yet for several years this area had been under the control of the Viet Minh, it seemed strange that they'd left one of the hated French colonialists unmolested.

"Who the hell are you?" I asked him abruptly.

"My name is Joseph Deville, Sergeant. And you are?"

"Sergeant Hoffman, Monsieur. French Foreign Legion, we are on a routine patrol of this area."

"They don't send many French soldiers around here," he commented.

"Really," I commented innocently. "This is a French colony, why should there not be French soldiers here?"

He realised instantly that he'd made a mistake and immediately tried to cover it.

"Of course, as a citizen of France I'm always happy to welcome our soldiers to my home. Please, come to the veranda at the back of the house, it's cooler.

"Trinh," he shouted. A Viet girl came out of the house. She was about eighteen, her pretty face marred with a set of buck teeth. She looked at us coldly, clearly unhappy at the presence of soldiers here.

"Trinh, would you serve cold lemonade and some sandwiches on the veranda, please," Deville said.

She murmured something and disappeared back into the house.

"Come gentlemen," Deville indicated a path at the side of the house.

We followed him to a shaded patio, arranged with tables and chairs, and sat down. Trinh came out after a few minutes with a large tray of glasses and jugs of lemonade. Deville served us all with cold drinks while Trinh went back into the house for food. We sat down enjoying our unexpected refreshments, while I tried to find out more about this puzzling set up in the middle of the communist dominated jungle of Northern Indochina.

"How on earth were the materials brought here to build this house, Monsieur Deville?"

"Ah, we have a waterway on the northern side of the plantation," he replied.

"It was a small river but was widened during the twenties when the rubber trade was expanding. Since the war, of course, it's beginning to revert to its individual state. But it was wide enough then to allow small boats to come up river to bring the masonry and materials to construct the house and some of the surrounding buildings."

"So the rubber business is still profitable?" I asked him.

"A shadow of its former self I'm afraid, but I get by. You haven't introduced yourselves or the young lady, Sergeant. You are all French? Your accent is unusual."

"Ah yes, this is Doctor Helene Baptiste." Helene shook hands with him.

"Enchante, Mam'selle," he said.

"Monsieur Deville, thank you for your hospitality." she replied.

"The rest of us are not French," I interrupted. "We are mainly Germans, some North Africans." I was interested to see his reaction.

"Germans? But I thought that the SS…"

He stopped speaking, realising that he was about to give himself away.

"How did you know we were SS? French policy is that SS are not recruited into the Legion."

"I heard it somewhere, I can't remember who told me that former SS men were serving in the Legion," he stammered.

"That's interesting, you can't get much news in this remote part of the country," I replied.

"No, that's true, but I have a short wave radio, I do keep up with most things. Let me get you some cakes, Sergeant, I know that Trinh has just baked some."

He got up and almost ran into the house. I nodded to von Kessler.

"Follow him, Manfred, I don't trust him at all."

"No, I can smell Viet Minh all over this place, I'll go check him out," he said, disappearing quietly into the house.

I signalled to the men to be ready, but the atmosphere was sufficiently tense that they were already checking their weapons ready for action. As Manfred has said, the whole place reeked of Viet Minh.

A few minutes later we heard shouting, a loud commotion coming from inside the house. Before we could check it out, Manfred re-emerged, holding Trinh by the throat, his other arm pointing his pistol, the Luger he'd carried all through the Eastern Front campaign, at Deville.

"Poison, Jurgen, the bitch was sprinkling it all over the pretty little cakes she was preparing for us."

Trinh was struggling, although no match for von Kessler's strength. Her eyes blazed with hate. She spat at me, I moved to one side to let it fly past my face.

"You colonialist scum, we will drive you and your masters back into the sea, every last one of you. If you stay here, you will die."

"Is that so?" I answered her.

"Corporal Dubois, take her back into the house and find out how many Viet Minh are in the immediate locality. It's pointless just asking her, so you can use your usual methods. Laurent, go with him and give him a hand, I think she's a bit of a firebrand."

They took hold of the girl and dragged her back into the house, we heard her screaming her message of hate and death as they went. Then there was silence.

"What are they doing to her?" Helene asked me.

"Asking her some questions, that's all," I replied.

"Do you think she'll tell them anything?"

"Yes, I do," I said.

There was a scream, long, agonised and chilling.

"Jurgen, for God's sake, they're torturing her. Stop them."

"Do you want to leave here and walk into a Viet Minh ambush," I asked her, "get captured and raped by a horde of communist savages, then beaten to death for the crime of being white and French?"

She shook her head.

"Fine!" I snapped.

"In order to avoid that happening to any of us, we need to know their strength, disposition of forces, communications and anything else that will help us. I suggest you leave us to do our job, which in part is keeping you alive, Mademoiselle Baptiste."

She glared at me then stormed off.

"Friedrich," I said to Sergeant Bauer, "follow her, make sure she doesn't get into trouble."

He nodded and strolled after the very angry, but beautiful young Frenchwoman. I turned to Deville.

"I think you have some explaining to do, Deville."

He smiled and spread his hands ingratiatingly.

"You must understand, Sergeant…"

He was interrupted by more piercing screams of agony from inside the house. Clearly Trinh was making Bruno Dubois work hard for the information.

"No, you must understand," I told him. "I know that you're collaborating with the Viet Minh, I know that you were helping Trinh to poison my men. Now, quickly, how many Viet Minh are there in this area?"

"Sergeant, how would I know? They don't tell me anything."

"Manfred, go and tell them to bring out the girl."

"Yes, Jurgen. Right away."

A few minutes later he came back with Laurent and Renaud, carrying the girl Trinh between them. She was not a pretty sight, covered in blood, one arm hanging limply from its socket and several of her teeth missing. One of her eyes was closed, her face black and blue. Deville went even whiter than before.

"Any luck?" I asked Dubois. He shook his head, "No, Jurgen, she's a stubborn one."

"Right then, shoot her," I told him.

He pulled out his pistol, a MAC Mle 1950. It was a gun he had acquired recently and was very proud of.

The MAC-50, also known as the MAC 1950, PA modèle 1950, was a standard semi-automatic pistol popular in the French army and the Legion. Adopted in 1950, it replaced the previous series of French pistols, the Modèle 1935A & Modèle 1935S, and was produced between 1950 and 1970. It used the Browning system with an integral barrel feed ramp, a single-action trigger with slide mounted safety that locks the firing pin so that the hammer could be lowered by pressing the trigger with safety engaged.

A useful gun, I thought, as I looked on. I doubted that Trinh was much interested in the details of our standard issue side-arm.

He held it to Trinh's head and looked at me. I nodded. He pulled the trigger, there was a loud report and a spout of blood shot out of the girl's head. She crashed to the ground, lying in a mess of brains and blood. I turned back to Deville.

"Now, my friend, you were telling me about the Viet Minh in this area. How many are there working on this plantation, first of all?"

Within minutes we had all the information that he knew. There were ten Viets working on the rubber plantation, as well as the newly deceased Trinh. They were all working on the trees, seven men and three women. Normally they didn't carry weapons while they were at work, although they would all be well aware of our arrival and may have armed themselves in the meantime.

I sent Schuster out with four men to notify our sentries, Armand and Renaud, then to hunt them down. The rest of us moved into the house and took up position by the windows.

"Sergeant, I've done everything I could to help you, you know how difficult my position is here, living and working with these savages," Deville said to me.

"Indeed I do understand," I replied.

"Dubois," I nodded at the Arab then gazed at Deville. "Finish him."

"No," he screamed, then his scream was cut off as Dubois's pistol blew half his head away.

"I think that'll ease his difficulties," I said to them.

I saw Bauer rushing towards the house, propelling Helene along. There was a fusillade of shots from within the trees then the steady crack, crack, as the sniper rifles opened up. Bauer dashed in with the girl, who gasped at the sight of Deville's body.

"Viet Minh, Jurgen, ten of them. They've armed themselves with Mosin Nagants and were taking pot shots at us, but Armand and Renaud have already knocked down half of them. Schuster's got them pinned down in a wooden hut, I think they can take care of them, the last thing I saw was them setting up an MG 42."

"That should do it, Friedrich. Would you take care of Mam'selle Baptiste, the rest of you, come with me."

We went quickly towards the sound of the firing. Through a group of trees there were several wooden huts, undoubtedly accommodation for the plantation workers. Bullets buzzed around us as the Viets were shooting at anything they thought might be a target, but they weren't trained soldiers, not a single shot came even close. Schuster's men were in cover behind what looked like a storage shed. Nearer the hut occupied by the enemy was a stone wall. I could see two of our people, Fuchs and Fassbinder, setting up the MG 42 ready to go into action. They snapped in the belt, Fassbinder lay at the side of the gun ready to feed in the ammunition, Fuchs lay behind it and looked around for the order. They were ready, Schuster shouted to them.

"Kill the bastards, Klaus, every last one of them."

I was surprised at his vehemence. Normally he wasn't so emotional. He noticed my expression.

"They nearly had us, Jurgen, bastards were waiting in ambush. If they were any good they could have done a lot of damage."

"You must be getting old, Paul," I laughed. Then the machine gun opened up, the familiar 'buzz saw' sound shattering the last vestiges of peace from the day. Birds flew into the air as the rounds poured out of the gun. The hut was shredded by thousands of the steel jacketed bullets so that we began to see sunlight streaming through the holes. One by one the enemy ceased fire, until there was only silence from inside the hut. I shouted for the cease fire then we walked forward to inspect the damage. There was no need to enter the hut, the MG 42 had torn huge holes in the woodwork through which we could see inside. There were ten bodies, seven men and three women as Deville had said, although it was difficult to separate the sexes, the bodies were so destroyed by the massive firepower of the German made medium machine gun.

"They may as well have sheltered behind a table cloth," Schuster said drily.

"True," I replied. "Did we take any casualties?"

"None," he told me. "But it was a close thing."

He was still shaken, I wondered was he perhaps truly getting too old for this game. Or maybe we were too old, we'd been fighting since 1939, nearly fourteen years. For twelve of those years we'd been fighting the communists. We were no longer the optimistic young men we once were, ready to leap into action at the least provocation, ever ready to defend the honour of our unit as well as our comrades' lives. We were getting older, most soldiers would have been retired from active service long before now.

It was ironic, the Third Reich had treated the Jews as non-persons, untermensch. Now we were the pariahs of Europe, exiled to this jungle hell to endlessly fight the communists. We were almost like the ghost crew of the fabled Flying Dutchman, condemned to roam the world's battlegrounds for all eternity. But we were not ghosts, we were men. In truth most of us were getting tired and tired men made mistakes. I wondered how long we would be able to continue this lethal game of death before eventually the game itself took us as its prize. I shrugged off the morbid thought, I was a soldier and I had a job to do.

We regrouped at the house, all of us still intact, together with Helene Baptiste who continued smarting at the bloodshed. She'd seen the Viet Minh at first hand in the village where we found her. I wondered what it would take to open her eyes to the realities of war, or perhaps she preferred to remain blind to the brutal excesses of the battlefield. She refused to meet my eyes, but just stood waiting in the middle of the column. I sent out Armand and Renaud to the point, after ten minutes I gave the signal and we moved off. Petrov came up to me.

"Jurgen, I found some plastique in one of the store rooms, it looked like the Viets were in the business of making explosive booby traps. I moved a box of the stuff into the house and rigged it to go up when someone goes in to investigate."

"Excellent, Nikolai," I replied. "That should take care of a few of them. Well done."

We pressed on towards Dong Khe, a major town that had been held by the Viet Minh for more than two years. Our intelligence reported that one of the Chu Luc units was stationed there.

The Chu Luc were the Viet Minh main force units. According to our reports they were becoming larger and better trained. Their combined strength comprised roughly a hundred thousand combatants in seventy battalions, with another thirty three battalions of regional forces. This totalled forty thousand men as well as sixty thousand local support personnel. Giap had been using these Chu Luc main force units to harass French positions along the main routes in northern Indochina together with mines and ambushes.

We weren't equipped to take on a Viet Minh company, let alone a Chu Luc main force. Our only chance was to keep our heads down and veer to the west of the town to avoid being seen. Already we had made too much noise with the destruction of the unit on the Thai Nguyen road, as well as the plantation we'd just left. I could only hope the enemy would put it all down to a search and destroy mission, and attach no special importance to it. By nightfall we were already skirting the town, keeping ten kilometres to the west. There was no sign of the enemy and we made camp in the middle of a dense patch of jungle.

The humidity was very high, in the morning we were soaking wet and then discovered the leeches. We were covered in them. Their presence was made known by a shriek from Helene.

"Help, please, I'm covered in them! They're disgusting, Jurgen, get them off of me!"

SS to the rescue once more I thought, but wisely didn't voice my sentiment. I lit up a cigarette and began burning off the leeches as she cringed with horror and disgust.

"Aren't you covered in them?" she asked me."

"Certainly I am," I replied.

"Well, why not get yours removed?"

"Ladies first," I smiled.

She smiled back, thank God she was beginning to thaw. Her

next words confirmed it.

"Jurgen, I'm sorry, I behaved like a stupid girl back there. You've save my life on more than one occasion, I will try and understand that warfare is not a pleasant business. Why are the communists so brutal?"

I thought for a moment.

"Their warlord Ho Chi Minh was quoted as saying 'You can kill ten of my men for every one I kill of yours, but even at those odds, you will lose and I will win.'. That's the problem, you see. Their philosophy is that communism is everything, people are nothing. The communists brutally execute hundreds of French officials, teachers, Buddhist monks and Catholic priests in their drive to bring the people around to their way of thinking. Clearly marked hospitals have been blown away by Viet Minh artillery fire, in the name of the cause. Massacre after massacre, they use rockets against densely populated areas, including refugee centres. Their execution procedure is nauseating. A Viet Minh unit rounds up citizens of a village for a "people's court" trial. Village chiefs, their deputies and anyone determined as connected with the French government are shot."

I looked at her, saw the horror in her eyes and decided to drive home the realities of war in Indochina.

"Other prisoners are labelled with tags, just as the Jews were marked with the Star of David in Hitler's concentration camps. Those Viets considered friendly to the communist cause get green tags; neutrals, yellow; and pro-French red. Some of the red-tagged are given dirty jobs to perform and if they get out of line, they're immediately shot. Next of kin can also be executed. The wife of a deputy subsector commander was condemned for "crimes against the people". She was publicly butchered, her body cut into three pieces by the Communists. They have become the Nazis of Indochina, killing and butchering as they wage war and retreat. And no, before you mention it, I was never in fact a Nazi."

She made no reply, and I decided enough was enough. I finished removing her leeches then went and found a discreet bush where I could strip and remove my own. The other men were doing the same. I smiled at their discretion where a pretty girl was concerned. Then we were ready, Armand and Renaud moved off and shortly we formed up and followed. Within two hours Renaud came running back down the path.

"Viet Minh, Sergeant, Armand is watching them. It seems to be some sort of a prison camp."

"Right, I'll come and take a look. Friedrich, take over, Renaud, come with me. The rest of you wait here and keep out of sight."

We went quietly up the path for about a kilometre, turned into a smaller path and then the camp came into view. It was a dismal collection of wooden huts, hidden beneath the jungle canopy, about a hundred metres off of the main path. It was so well concealed that if Armand and Renaud hadn't heard voices coming from the camp they could have walked straight past it.

The camp was surrounded by barbed wire strung on poles. The wire had even been woven over the roof of the camp, making it impossible to climb over and out of the camp without cutting through the wire. There were four guards lined up in a central square of hard packed earth, all armed with Soviet Mosin Nagant rifles. They were being supervised by an officer, a short, fat Viet armed with a pistol which he used to emphasise his shouted commands. He seemed to have got out of bed the wrong side. Renaud confirmed that it was his shouting that had alerted them first to the presence of the camp. The windows to the huts were enclosed with what looked like iron bars. There were no prisoners in evidence, but certainly they were not too far away, the barbed wire was there for a purpose. Then the officer stopped shouting and the soldiers ran to a low lying structure in the centre of the square. They slid back some huge bolts and two of them lifted the heavy hatch that covered what appeared to be a hole in the ground. One of them, presumably an NCO, began screaming orders. Almost immediately men began appearing, ragged, emaciated scarecrows, climbing out of the hatch and standing to some semblance of attention in the square. There were nine of them altogether, all white men, obviously French prisoners. I got out my binoculars and looked more closely, it was possible to make out the badges on their uniforms. They were all officers.

There was more shouting and the poor devils were marched away to a store, where they picked up tools and went off into the jungle. It looked as if they were on a wood cutting detail. Three of the guards accompanied them, one stayed and stood guard at the gate.

The prisoners were in a terrible state covered in sores, ragged and filthy dirty. All of them looked as if they were suffering from several of the common ailments that the jungle inflicted on soldiers of all armies, and which untreated meant lingering painful misery, often resulting in death. The officer went into the guard hut, where we heard him shouting at some-one, presumably a further soldier, probably his clerk. So there were six of the enemy in total, the officer, his clerk and four others. We went quietly back down the track, leaving Renaud to watch the camp, and I described the scene to the men.

"Common sense dictates that we leave them there, but somehow it goes against the grain to do that. I've never left a man in the hands of the savages before and I don't intend to start now. The question is, how do we organise this without alerting the Viet Minh?"

After a brief silence, Schuster spoke.

"Suppose they were to desert, or at least simply disappear? If we can leave everything tidy the Viets will just think their men disappeared, or maybe had orders to move the prisoners elsewhere."

I thought about it for a few moments.

"Excellent, that's probably our best shot. At the very least it will leave an element of doubt."

"What about the prisoners?" Bauer asked.

"They're in no shape to come with us, Friedrich. The best we can do is tend to their wounds as best we can. Helene, can you do anything with them?"

"Of course," she said.

"That's it then, we'll leave the prisoners with our spare radio and as much food and supplies as we can spare. We'll ask them to give us a day's start then they can radio for an evacuation. I suggest we attack the camp after dark. Remember, we need to be very careful not to leave any evidence of a firefight. Corporal Dubois, you can take out the gate guard first."

The Arab smiled. "With pleasure, Sergeant."

"Right that's it then. We'll use the rest of the daylight to move into position, Friedrich."

I said to Bauer.

"Take four men and one of the MG 42s, make your way around to the north of the camp. Paul, bring three men and the other machine gun and come with me, we'll close in ready to take out the guards. Try to avoid using the machine guns unless it's absolutely necessary. Private Fuchs, stay here with Mam'selle Baptiste and make sure she's safe."

We got up and left and within an hour were safely under cover, watching the camp. Just before dark the prisoners were marched back and herded into one of the barred huts. A guard took one of the prisoners into another hut, presumably the kitchen, and he came out shortly afterwards carrying a full bucket. The evening meal, no doubt! He went to the prisoners' hut and when he came out the door was locked solidly behind him. The guards seemed to relax now that their charges were safely locked away for the night, they stood around smoking and chatting, one of them brought out a bottle and they cheerfully passed it around. The officer came out of his hut, together with a young soldier who was carrying his boots and sat down to begin polishing them. One of the soldiers ran to get a chair for the officer, who sat down and pulled a letter out of his pocket which he began to read carefully. I assumed it was a letter from home. It would be the last one he ever received.

We waited quietly as dusk crept over the jungle. The camp

wasn't equipped with electricity. One of the guards went around lighting oil lamps then rejoined his comrades, drinking and smoking. The officer went inside with his clerk and the men pulled out more bottles and began drinking heavily. Inside of an hour they were all semi-comatose, it was time. I signalled to Dubois who crept down to the gate. I could just make him out through the gloom. There was a 'clink' as he threw a stone that hit the ground just outside of the fence, near to the guard. His head whipped around, and he peered into the darkness. Seeing nothing, he opened the gate and walked to the source of the noise, his rifle at the ready. I saw a shadow move then the guard struggled briefly and was lowered to the ground. Dubois reappeared shortly afterwards.

"All clear, Sergeant. He's dead."

"Ok. Men, let's move in quietly and dispose of the rest of them."

We crept down to the camp through the open gate and moved from hut to hut until we were close to the three guards.

"Dubois, you lead, the rest of you use your bayonets, no shooting if you can avoid it."

Dubois looked around the end of the hut then turned to us.

"They're looking away, we can take them now if we're quick."

Without waiting for an acknowledgement he sped around the corner, I followed and saw him run up to the first soldier and slice the man's throat. I had my bayonet out, grabbed the next man around the mouth to stop him crying out then stabbed the point into the man's heart. Almost immediately he slumped, dead. Two of my men had taken the third guard, one held him while the other, imitating Dubois, pulled a knife across his throat. There was a sigh of escaping air and the last of the three dropped dead at our feet.

Paul Schuster was watching the officer's hut carefully, his submachine gun, a MAT 49, cocked and ready to open fire if the man or his clerk appeared. All was quiet, however, and shortly we were joined by Friedrich Bauer and his men, who crept noiselessly into the camp. I walked up to the door and tried the handle, it was unlocked. I gently opened it into an office in semi-darkness. There was a half-opened door on the opposite side of the room, through which a soft light was shining through sufficiently for us to see inside, presumably the sleeping quarters. We crept quietly across the office and I looked cautiously into the next room. Sure enough, it was a bedroom. The tubby little Viet officer was naked on the bed, vigorously sodomising the naked man, his clerk, who lay on the bed below him.

I walked boldly into the room, there was no real need for stealth, these two were totally preoccupied with what they were doing. I reversed my MP38 and hit the fat man on the head, knocking him out cold. Dubois came up next to me and took the clerk's neck in his hands and began to squeeze, tighter and tighter. He struggled, tried to call out, trying to prise the Arab's hands away, but gradually he became weaker as his air supply was cut off and he finally fell dead.

"Paul, tie up the fat one, you can fasten him to the chair in the office, the prisoners may want a word with him. Bruno, a good job, well done, get some of the men and release the prisoners."

152

Bauer came up to me.

"I've sent a man to bring in Mam'selle Baptiste and Private Fuchs. Armand and Renaud are guarding the gate."

"Thank you, Friedrich."

Karl-Heinz and Manfred had already broken off the padlocks from the huts, the prisoners were coming out into the gloomy night. Even in the dark they looked far, far worse than when I'd watched them earlier through the binoculars. Two of them had legs that were crooked, broken at some stage and never properly set. They stank of faeces, urine, vomit and filth. Nonetheless, we embraced them warmly, our fellow soldiers. It turned out they were officers of the Colonial Infantry, captured when their posts had been overrun by the Viet Minh. Their men had been killed horrifically, even after laying down their arms in surrender. The officers were kept for possible future use as hostages, and spent their days alternating between manual labour and hours spent locked in the hole in the square as punishment for any infraction dreamed up by their Viet Minh captors. When they found out we had the officer captive, they were overjoyed. Two of them rushed away to find him and pay him back for some of the extreme cruelty they'd suffered. It was going to be an interesting session.

We checked around the camp and managed to replenish some of our supplies of food and ammunition from the stores. The screams had already started and they went on for what seemed like an eternity, but was probably no more than fifteen minutes. Abruptly, they stopped. The prisoners came out of the hut and walked across to us.

"My name is Michel Bellaire, I am the senior French officer

in this camp, my rank is colonel. On behalf of my men, I want to extend my deepest thanks to you for rescuing us from this hell. Including myself there are only nine of us left. Originally I commanded three companies on a search and destroy mission, we were ambushed by the Viet Minh. I was in charge of a March Battalion, my men were mainly Algerian riflemen, all regulars. They took a hundred and ninety three of us into captivity, we are all that's left."

"What happened to the rest of you?" I asked the Colonel.

"Executions, starvation, disease, all of it avoidable. They treated us worse than animals. Even now, some of my survivors are in bad shape. Have you come from Hanoi to rescue us? How did you find out we were here?"

I had to explain that we were on a mission and had only chanced on the camp by accident.

"I'm sorry Colonel, much as I am concerned to get you back to Hanoi as quickly and safely as possible, the mission we're on is of immense importance to our war effort. I'm afraid we're going to have to find somewhere for you to wait for a rescue. Staying in the camp is obviously out of the question, we have no idea when the Viet Minh may arrive to check that everything is in order."

The Colonel was obviously taken aback, but still overwhelmed with joy at being rescued from the Viets.

"No," he said. "Staying here is definitely not an option, they come through about twice a week with supplies and check the number of survivors. They were here yesterday so we have a couple of days start on them before their next visit, but when they do come back we need to be as far away as possible."

I called Friedrich Bauer and we went over the maps. Eventually we found a trail close by that would lead the Frenchman in a westerly direction, away from the camp and the line of march that we were taking to Cao Bang. I pointed it out to Colonel Bellaire and he examined the map carefully while he munched on some of the food Vogelmann and Kessler had given him and the rest of the prisoners. Helene was going round with our rapidly diminishing medical supplies, tending to some of the wounds and running sores whilst giving all the prisoners antibiotic injections to ward off the worst of the infections they were all suffering from.

"Yes, that definitely looks like a possibility," the Colonel murmured.

"Exactly how far do you want us to travel before we attempt to make contact with Hanoi? The Viets captured some of our field radios when they took us, occasionally they get them out to listen for broadcasts from any units in the area. We can take one of those with us and call in an evacuation as soon as we're sufficiently far away."

I would have liked them to travel at least fifty kilometres before they started to broadcast on the open airwaves. It was inevitable that as soon as they did broadcast the Viet Minh would pick it up and would go and check the source of the radio message. At the same time, there was no way that these men were going to walk that far and still be alive to make the call.

"Do you think you can manage twenty kilometres, Colonel?"

Bellaire thought for a moment.

"I think so, it will take us a couple of days but yes, we can manage it. I intend to travel as far as possible at first light and get away from here, just in case the Viets do return. We can rest and eat some of the food, then see how much progress we can make. Yes, we can do it."

I left the Colonel and went around the camp supervising the hiding of any evidence that we'd been there. The men carried each of the bodies into the jungle and buried them, where it was unlikely they would be discovered in the near future. In the morning we double checked to make certain there was no evidence of our being at the camp. Then we said our goodbyes to the Frenchmen, left them with one of our maps and as many of our dwindling supplies as we could manage and got back on the trail to Cao Bang.

We fell into the usual order of march, with two men on the point, a further two covering our rear and Helene Baptiste in the middle of the column. There was little to say, the very idea of an entire March Battalion being reduced to the nine pitiful men we had released was hard to swallow, yet it was by no means unique. Since the fall of China when Mao Tse Tung had begun supplying arms and equipment to the communists in Indochina, the French had been suffering increasing losses and Colonel Bellaire's Battalion was by no means unique in being virtually wiped out by a clever and well equipped enemy.

It was certainly something to ponder and seeing more evidence of Viet Minh savagery, combined with their increasing military successes, amounted to a solid argument for an early end to the war in Indochina. I discussed it with Paul Schuster, who was walking alongside me.

"We've been here before, Jurgen," he said.

"It's not so long ago that the Fuhrer totally underestimated the communists in Russia and sent hundreds of thousands of our soldiers to their deaths. It was reckless stupidity, I thought I would never live to see it again, yet I wonder is this not history repeating itself?"

"We're all beginning to think along the same lines, Paul," I replied.

"It makes this mission to assassinate Giap that much more important. If we can take the bastard out of the equation it may make things a lot easier for us."

"Will it?" he asked. "Do you honestly think that, Jurgen?"

"I have to," I told him.

"I have to take responsibility for the men and for the mission, I need something to believe in. It may not win the war but yes, it will give us much more of a chance of bringing them to the negotiating table. That in itself would at least shorten the war."

"I hope so, Jurgen," he said. "I truly hope so."

CHAPTER SEVEN

We picked up the pace, trying to reach Cao Bang before the Viets started to investigate our activities. I firmly believed the rescue at the prison camp could be the final piece in the jigsaw that an intelligent Viet commander could put together and work out that a French force was engaged on some kind of the mission in the area. We soon left the Viet tribal area that constituted the largest ethnic group in Northern Indochina and entered the area of the Nung people.

The group was the sixth largest of Vietnam's fifty three minority groups, with a population of nearly nine hundred thousand and it had local groups, Nung Xuong, Nung Giang, Nung An, Nung Phan Sinh, Nung Loi, Nung Tung Slin, Nung Chao and many others. They were considered to have retained more of their traditional culture, and were less open to outside influences. Large numbers of the Nung had in fact recently fled across the border from China when Mao Tse Tung overran the country with his communist revolution. Many had fled further south to the region around Saigon, but even more had settled in Northern Indochina, especially around the area of Cao Bang.

There was no question that we could trust the Nung any more than the Vietnamese, the whole area had been totally subjugated by the communists. However, the communists like any other people had strong tribal instincts. The largest ethnic group were the Vietnamese who would of course favour their own people where the distribution of resources was concerned. This would mean that the Nung tribe may not be fully in the pay of the communists and I hoped to be able to gain some kind of intelligence about the current situation at Giap's HQ.

We were soon to find out, as our point men reported that we were approaching the outskirts of Dong Khe, the largest town before we reached Cao Bang itself. We left the track and moved into the jungle, within two hundred metres we found ourselves on the edge of a lake. It was a natural point to make camp, well screened from passing traffic and obviously we could replenish our water supplies. The men gratefully shrugged off their packs and sat down, dragging out rations and preparing a meal while they had the chance. Before I could decide on my next move, Helene Baptiste came up to me and offered to help.

"Jurgen, I know this area, I was in Dong Khe on my previous assignment. I still have contacts there, if you wish I can see what I can find out."

It was a tempting offer, but Dong Khe would inevitably have a strong Viet Minh presence and the idea of Helene Baptiste walking in to have a friendly word with one of her contacts was not very attractive. I explained this to her, but she was insistent.

"The thing is, I was very friendly with an old Buddhist priest who helped to run the hospital on the southern outskirts of the town. I got to know him well, I'm certain I could reach him and he would be happy to help us. He was certainly no friend of the communists, that I can assure you."

I thought about this, any local knowledge would be of tremendous value to us. One of our overriding concerns was the consistently out of date intelligence our own people supplied. It was no substitute for having a man with his ear to the ground. Eventually I relented, provided that she was escorted. I assigned Corporal Vogelmann and Private Fuchs to accompany her.

"A little further along the track there's a path that branches off and leads to the hospital," Helene told me.

"There shouldn't be any problem getting in there unseen."

"I hope so," I replied.

"Karl-Heinz, Private Fuchs, leave your heavy weapons here, it's pistols only I'm afraid. I don't want any of the locals to see heavily armed troops in the area, so try and be discreet."

"We're always discreet, Jurgen," Vogelmann laughed.

"Keep it that way then," I told him. "Good luck, men."

They set off back to the main track and headed in the direction of Dong Khe. We sat around and chatted quietly. There was little else to do until they came back, hopefully with some useful information that would help us to reach Cao Bang safely and complete our mission. In the distance I could see the hills that led to the Chinese border, less than fifty kilometres away.

It was a beautiful area. The Nung people were horticulturalists and the regions around Dong Khe and Cao Bang were covered in the evidence of their rural lives. The terraces were carefully tended with a variety of crops and unusually hundreds of ponds that they used for a fairly advanced form of fish farming.

The importance to the Viet Minh of this area could not be underestimated. There was no doubt that they would be imposing heavy taxes on foodstuffs to the local people, which they would in turn use to sustain their guerrilla armies.

The more I thought about it the more anxious I became. They wouldn't leave such an important strategic reserve without strong defences. As the hours dragged by I wondered if I should send a couple of men to find out what had happened to them. I went to speak to Manfred Kessler but before I could order him to get ready to leave, Helene returned with her two escorts. They also had with them a young woman, wearing traditional Nung costume resplendent with the silver jewellery that they loved to display.

"Good news," Vogelmann said.

"The old priest was a veritable mine of information. It seems that the Viet Minh have turned the whole population into virtual slaves. Their property has been confiscated and turned over to the party for feeding the troops, in return the Nung are allowed to live on the land and continue to work it. They absolutely detest the communists and can't wait to see the French impose some sort of order on the place."

"Who is the girl?" I asked him.

"Her name's Pham, she's related to the priest. She occasionally goes to Cao Bang to buy jewellery and knows the area very well. She's volunteered to come with us."

"Manfred, why the hell would she offer to come with us on a military mission? She could get killed."

"She knows the risks, Jurgen. Her brother was conscripted by the Viet Minh to help them carry their supplies. When he refused to go they made him kneel down and then put a bullet through his head in front of the whole family. She wants to do something to hit back at them, believe me, Pham is totally committed to us."

I wasn't happy about taking an unknown civilian with us. It was enough that we had Helene Baptiste with us, but at least she was French and had been held captive by the Viet Minh. We had no doubts about her loyalty. Pham may well be the genuine article, but there was really no way of knowing.

"Does she speak any French?"

"Pham speaks French fluently," Helene said to me. "She also of course speaks the native Nung language, so she'll be very valuable to us."

I looked at her, she was a pretty enough girl of about twenty. Helene was quite correct, with her local knowledge and ability to speak Nung, she could indeed prove to be very valuable. If on the other hand she was not genuine, she could be the instrument of our deaths. In the end I agreed that she should come with us, but told Friedrich Bauer to put the word around that she was to be watched very carefully and not trusted, at least for the time being.

"Pham," I called to her.

"How long will it take us to reach Cao Bang, and do you

know of a route we can take that'll keep us off of the main track?"

"If we take the path over the hillside we can reach Cao Bang in about two hours, Sergeant." she said.

"Are we likely to meet anyone on that path?" I asked her.

"No, no, I don't think there'll be any Viet Minh in that area."

"What about civilians?" I continued.

"I don't think so, no, no civilians."

I wasn't totally convinced by her replies, Dong Khe and Cao Bang were big areas and surrounded by a large number of farms and settlements. Still, I accepted that we had to give it a try on the basis of what she said. I gave the orders and we put on our packs, picked up our weapons and left for the final stage of our journey.

We'd only travelled for a few hundred metres along the track towards Dong Khe before Pham directed us to yet another small path that led into the hills. I kept up a hard pace, wanting to arrive at Cao Bang before nightfall. Within three hours, just as dusk was falling, we were approaching the outskirts of the town. The path ran past a waterfall, a natural beauty spot that Pham assured us was rarely visited by the Viets. We made camp there by the side of the lake, just under the waterfalls and out of sight of any casual passerby. I set out pickets and then sat to eat an evening meal.

The food was fairly unappetising, consisting of the last of our dried food supplemented by some rice and pickled vegetables we'd taken from the prison camp. I asked Pham what she knew about Cao Bang.

Certainly the whole area had been central to the communist uprising and in 1950 Ho Chi Minh and Giap managed to gather enough forces in the area to defeat the French and take control. Outside Cao Bang there were several cave systems, many of which had been used by the communists as hidden barracks in which to keep troops hidden from the French.

"The communists are in full control of the town, Sergeant. For the peasants, there is no life. They force us to work for them and everything that we make or grow is heavily taxed. If anyone protests, like my brother, they are killed."

I didn't want to give her any idea why we were in the area. It would be best if she thought that we were purely on a reconnaissance mission.

"Do you know where the communists have their headquarters?" I asked.

"Certainly, they've taken over a building in the town, but the men in command stay in a villa which is outside of the town. It has been overgrown by the jungle since it was abandoned by the French many years ago, so it's impossible to see from the air, but everyone in the village knows where it is. Many of us have to go and work there for the communists, I've been there to clean and to take food for the kitchens."

I was itching to ask her the million dollar question. Was Giap there? But it was impossible without giving away the object of our mission. Finally, I drifted off to sleep, lulled into a relaxed state by the sound of the water cascading down the waterfall.

I woke up before dawn and gathered the men to prepare for the final stage of the journey. We were about to enter the tiger's lair, the holy of holies of Ho Chi Minh's chief executioner, Nguyen Giap, the supposedly military genius and certainly the architect of the Viet Minh victories over the French the year before. Not only that, our mission was to either kidnap him if that was possible, or as seemed more likely, assassinate him and then escape with our lives.

What had seemed like a distinct possibility in the safety of the barracks in Hanoi now seemed to be virtually impossible. We had no idea how many troops were stationed in the area, but it was known to be a training and supply centre for several of the Viet Minh chu lucs, the main battle formations that Giap sent against us in set piece attacks. I asked Pham if it would be at all possible to approach the villa where the senior officers lived without being seen.

"Yes Sergeant, I think it should be possible but it depends on the number of patrols the communists have out. Sometimes the soldiers go away and the area is fairly quiet, at other times there are many soldiers and we hear much shooting around the hills and the jungle. I think they must be training. Although I live in Dong Khe I haven't seen many soldiers there lately. So yes, there is a good chance. I can definitely lead you on a path through the jungle that will avoid the checkpoints."

"Tell me about these checkpoints, how many soldiers guard them, what sort of weapons do they carry?"

Pham looked perplexed.

"I'm sorry, Sergeant, I don't understand. They carry rifles like you do. There are usually three or four soldiers at each checkpoint."

"And how many checkpoints are there likely to be around the villa?" I asked her.

"I honestly don't know," she said.

"I don't usually look around when I go to the villa, I just do my work and leave as quickly as possible. Would you like me to go and find out?"

"How on earth could you do that? If you were caught you would be killed."

She looked me straight in the eye.

"What you need to understand, Sergeant, is that these vermin killed my brother just because he wouldn't help them. I would do anything, anything at all to drive them out of my country. The communists have already driven the Nung people out of China, many of us settled here hoping to live a normal life. Now they have come here too. Many of our people have fled once more to the south of the country around Saigon, but there are still many more of us who would just like to be left in peace. Anything I can do that will strike a blow against the communists will help bring about the time when we can once more live normal lives."

It was an impressive speech. I began to have more confidence in her and to understand the horrors that had driven her to want to take such chances. Certainly the Nung had been treated harshly by Mao Tse Tung's communists after the revolution and now they seemed to be suffering the same fate here in their new home of Indochina. Perhaps with a few more like Pham the communists would think twice before they tried to take over the whole country.

"What excuse would you have to go there?"

"That's not a problem, Sergeant. Apart from food and weapons, one of their main requirements is a supply of whores. If

I pretend to be going there as one they will not question me."

It was a fearful dilemma. On the one hand the intelligence she could gain from going to the villa would be priceless and could make all the difference between success or failure of our mission. On the other hand, if they caught her she would be killed, but if she was a traitor... well, that would be the end of us. She could sell us out to the communists and earn a substantial reward for her treachery.

I called Friedrich Bauer over and we walked off to discuss it. In the end, I agreed that she would go and pose as a whore to find out what kind of odds we would be up against. We also decided, in the interests of our safety, to move our camp once she'd left so that if she did sell us out to the Viets, they would only find an empty camp when they came looking for us.

Eventually, Pham departed for the officers' villa. We gave her ten minutes then packed up the camp, clearing the area as best we could to hide any evidence of our being there, and moved off over the hill where we could wait for her. Armand and Renaud took up a position where they could keep an eye on our old camp and watch for Pham returning. Our new camp was in a deep bamboo thicket, difficult to approach except for a narrow channel we'd hacked through. The insects gave us hell and we spent three miserable hours covering ourselves with ointment and using every means possible to drive them away. Even so, by the time we heard a quiet call from Armand to announce their return, we were covered in insect bites and more than pleased to be able to move out. Pham was with them, but her appearance was terrible. Her face was covered in bruises and her clothes were ripped, her eyes wide with fear.

Helene rushed out to her.

"My dear, what happened to you?" she asked her.

"Pham, did they catch you?" I added.

"No," she replied bitterly.

"They didn't catch me, I offered myself to them as a whore for money. At least, that's what I told them. But they weren't interested in paying. They took me to the villa and held me down while they took turns raping me."

We were all silent. War was brutal, and this particular war in Indochina seemed to be characterised by far more brutality than most. Even on the Eastern Front, where the behaviour of the troops took barbarism to new levels of depravity, I couldn't envisage our senior officers kidnapping and then gang raping a young girl, some of the ordinary troops of both armies perhaps, but the senior officers? No, never. It was a sober reminder to us all that the enemy we were dealing with was like nothing we had dealt with before.

I spent some time questioning Pham about the route to the villa and the layout inside. It was a typical French plantation villa on two floors. There was a huge lounge in the downstairs area which the occupants use as a kind of officers' mess. There were also kitchens and other staff quarters on the ground floor. Upstairs were the bedrooms, apparently there were about ten of them, for the senior officers.

"If you go now, Sergeant, you would certainly find them unprepared. Most of them are currently entertaining their whores," she said bitterly.

It was time to ask the only question that really mattered.

"Pham, do you know if Comrade Giap is at the villa? Do

you know who I mean?"

"Yes, I know him," Pham replied.

"He's a very cruel man, he treats us worse than any of the others. When I was leaving one of the guards was dragging two girls into the house, I overheard him say that they were to entertain Comrade Giap." She shuddered.

It was the best possible news we could hear. If we could grab Giap, or kill him as a last resort, everything else would be worthwhile.

"How many guards are there around the villa, inside and out?" I asked.

She thought for a moment.

"I think there are about eight of the Nung people acting as servants to the Viets, as for soldiers, I would think about fifteen to twenty. I'm sorry, I cannot be precise."

"No, no, you've done very well, Pham. While we make the attack on the villa you must stay here with Helene."

"I wish to come with you, Sergeant, I want to have vengeance for my brother. If I can kill some Viet Minh it would be as much as I could ask from this life."

"Have you ever killed a man, Pham?" I asked her. "Killed a man close-up, with a knife, when you can look him in the eyes and see him breathe his last breath? Is that what you want?"

"Yes, Sergeant that's what I want."

She took out a knife, a wicked looking knife that she had probably used recently for finely chopping vegetables and slicing fish.

"I have my knife, please take me with you so that I can use it."

She was adamant that nothing less than payment in blood would be sufficient revenge for the execution of her brother. I decided to let her come with us. She could kick up a fuss if I tried to make her stay behind and besides she could be very useful as a guide to take us on the last stage of our journey. The villa was only a thirty minute hike away, we prepared our weapons as best we could and waited for dusk. We all rubbed charcoal over our faces to make it more difficult for the Viets to see us coming, but I hoped to catch them all unawares.

Finally dusk came down and Pham led the way towards the villa. I ordered Helene to walk near the back of the group, I would have preferred not to have taken her with us, but leaving her alone was not an option. For the first time, I began to regret my decision at allowing her to come along.

We all had our weapons ready but I made certain that they weren't cocked. It only needed one random shot to bring a division of Viet Minh troops down upon our heads. I called for Corporal Dubois to come to the front.

"Corporal, you're the best man in the Foreign Legion with a knife, you know what needs to be done?"

"Yes, Sergeant Hoffman. You want me to go ahead and dispose of the sentries without making any noise."

"Good man," I acknowledged him. "Wait for my order."

There was some light coming through the jungle canopy, it was almost a full moon but luckily the sky was very cloudy so that we didn't have to worry about bright moonlight betraying our positions. But it was enough light for us to see where we were going. Pham held up her hand and we all came to a stop and crouched down. I edged forward and could clearly see the

Viet Minh house through the trees. It was an isolated structure surrounded by several outhouses and a wire fence. There was a gatehouse at the entrance to the compound with a lifting barrier across it. Next to the barrier a guard was standing quietly smoking, talking to someone else who was just out of sight.

The men crouched down, waiting in the darkness. Apart from the usual jungle noises, everything seemed quite. A little music was coming from the villa, someone had a radio or a gramophone playing. I turned to Corporal Dubois.

"Dubois, you can take Renaud with you, go now. Remember, no noise."

"Yes, Sergeant. Xavier, come here."

Renaud came forward, another North African who was as familiar with using a knife as blowing his nose.

"Yes, Corporal."

"You take the guard standing by the barrier, I'll go for the other one that we can't see. Keep it quiet, there may be others in the guard hut, we'll need to deal with them too."

The two men crept quietly forward, soon they were lost in the gloom. Suddenly a figure appeared next to the guard I could see, there was a slight movement, the Viet guard was dragged into the guard hut. I heard the beginnings of a cry, that was quickly stifled, then silence. After a few minutes, Dubois and Renaud came out of the hut and reported back.

"All clear, Sergeant. There was just one other guard in the hut, he was half asleep so we put him out of his misery. The bodies are all out of sight."

"Well done," I replied. "You all know what to do, let's go."

We slipped into the grounds of the villa, past the now deserted guard hut. I posted two guards to watch for any new arrivals, then the men followed me into the building. Pham was with me, together with Vogelmann. A door opened in the hall and a Viet servant came out, he opened his mouth to shout, then dropped to the floor as Dubois' knife whistled across the room and buried itself in his throat. I nodded to the Arab corporal, who grinned back. I signalled at four of the men to take the ground floor rooms, the rest of us crept quietly up the stairs. We found ourselves on a long, spacious landing, with a dozen doors leading off of it. Friedrich Bauer and Dubois silently entered the first room, there was a slight sound and then they came out.

"One Viet, asleep in bed. Permanently," he added.

"Did you recognise him?" I whispered.

He shook his head. I went with Vogelmann to the end of the landing and opened a bedroom door.

We walked in and found ourselves face to face with Vo Nguyen Giap, commander of the communist forces, second in the hierarchy of the people's revolution, after Ho Chi Minh. He was naked, lying on the bed, next to him was a girl who looked to be no more than twelve years old. She saw his eyes widen and he whirled around, startled.

Vogelmann walked over and effortlessly lifted the girl off of the bed and dumped her on the floor. I put my finger to my lips, and pointed my MP38 at him, then walked over to the bed.

"Comrade Giap, if you make any noise, this gentleman will slit your throat so that you never make any noise ever again. Not one word, clear?"

He nodded, watching me carefully. He looked at Vogelmann, then his eyes darted around the room. Without a doubt, until we either killed him or got him away from here, we were in a very dangerous position. Silent, watchful, and ready to take advantage of the tiniest opportunity to turn the tables he tried, without success, to hide the face of the VietMinh military genius behind the archetypal mask of oriental inscrutability.

"Giap, get your clothes on," I ordered him. "Remember, dead or alive, it makes no difference. Make a sound and we'll leave your body here for your men to cry over."

He made no reply, just got slowly off of the bed and began dressing. As soon as he was ready, I tied his hands behind his back and whispered to Vogelmann to go and check the passage outside the door. As his hand was on the doorknob, we heard a shouted command from downstairs, then the beginning of an altercation.

Obviously someone from the Viet Minh guard knew we were here, things were about to warm up. Giap was doing his best not to smile, but his face betrayed him, a mixture of fear that he may be killed combined with pleasure that his captors were probably about to suffer the same fate.

I wondered how true he was to his cause. Would he practice what he preached, would he be happy to die to see the hated French colonisers destroyed? Or was that a sentiment reserved for other, lesser mortals. I suspected that like most military leaders, the latter would be the case. Brave, certainly, but dying in battle was for others to suffer.

Vogelmann peered out through the door. As he did so, there was a strangled cry of agony, then silence again. I whispered urgently to him.

"Karl-Heinz, go and see what's happening, I'll cover Giap."

He slipped quietly through the door. The racket downstairs was building, clearly some of the Viet Minh were alerted to our presence. Giap was doing his best to look inscrutable, but couldn't totally hide the triumph in his eyes, now that he thought we were discovered. Vogelmann came back.

"Jurgen, we've got trouble. About a dozen Viet Minh, some sort of a guard patrol. Four of them came into the house and we've finished them off, but the rest are outside waiting to hit us when we leave."

"And they will have called for reinforcements," I added.

He nodded. "Within ten minutes this place will be crawling with the bastards."

"Who will be reluctant to shoot at their commander. We have Giap, we'll use him to get out of here. Let's get moving. Comrade Giap, get downstairs."

We followed the Viet leader along the passage. Through open bedroom doors I could glimpse bodies lying on bloodied sheets, testifying to the death and terror we'd brought to this remote part of Indochina, an area where the enemy thought it was totally safe. At least we'd changed all of that.

The men were gathered in the hallway, waiting. Pham was holding a bloodied knife, obviously some of the victims in the bedrooms had been hers. Helene was bandaging a wound, I afterwards found out that the man went into the kitchen to investigate and got stabbed in the back for his pains.

Their eyes widened as they recognised Giap, the bogey man of the French colonialists for the past ten years. I pulled Giap to the front door.

"Comrade, we're leaving now. Tell your men to hold their fire or we'll put a bullet in your head. You will speak only in French, now do it."

I opened the door and pushed him out first onto the verandah. A small group of hostile looking Viets stood nearby, their weapons raised. As they saw Giap walk out of the door, their officer shouted a command and they lowered their guns. He kept his pistol trained on us, until I shouted at him.

"Lower your pistol. You men will not shoot. We have taken Giap prisoner and are keeping him with us until we can escape. When we are clear, we will release him. Men," I shouted to my troops, "come out now, we are leaving."

The men came out of the house, weapons raised, cocked, ready to fire. The air crackled with tension, I was well aware that the slightest spark would ignite the tinder box and the shooting would start. If hate could kill, the compound would be littered with bodies, I could sense both sides itching to start shooting, which would be the end of us all.

We were deep in the heart of Viet Minh territory, surrounded by tens of thousands of enemy soldiers. Our only hope was to get out of here as quickly as possible before they had time to work out a way to kill us, without killing Giap.

There was a sudden cry and Pham rushed forward, her bloody knife raised, she'd recognised the officer as one who had brutalised her earlier in the day. He was still holding his pistol, as she reached him he raised it and shot her in the chest. Her body jerked with the impact of the bullet, but her momentum carried her forward enough to plunge her knife into his groin. He collapsed on the ground, screaming in agony, blood spurting out of him in torrents. Pham fell backwards, dead, her mission of revenge over. Giap snapped out a command, one of his men went up to the fallen officer, put his rifle to the man's head and pulled the trigger. The bullet killed him instantly, silence once again descended on the compound. We were no strangers to killing, but Giap's casual order to silence the wounded officer, made under the guns of his French captors was a powerful illustration of the unlimited strength and resolve of this man.

"Giap, we're leaving, tell them to stay back. If we see a single weapon raised, you'll be shot."

"Men," I called.

"If one of them points a weapon our way, you will shoot Giap without further orders. Right, let's go. Helene, stay in the middle of the group."

We edged away from the house towards the gate. Vogelmann kept a hand on Giap, the other with his pistol held tight against the communist leader's head so that they didn't mistake the message. As we reached the gate, I spoke to Giap.

"Tell them not to follow or you will be killed."

He shouted to the Viets, who stood sullenly watching us leave. We went through the gate and found the path at the rear of the compound.

"We need to move very fast, there's no doubt they'll be following us. Friedrich, cover our rear with Fassbinder, make sure they don't get too close. The rest of you, double time, we need to be away from here before they bring up an entire regiment."

Bauer and Fassbinder dropped to the rear. I picked up the pace so that we were almost running along the jungle path.

We kept going for the next hour, dashing along the path, propelling our prisoner with us. We heard shooting in the rear and I sent Petrov back to investigate, but he reported back that it was only the Viets getting too near. Bauer and Fassbinder had fired a burst that hit two of them and convinced the others that we were serious.

As we ran, I contemplated the options. There was no way we would lose our pursuers. Giap was far too valuable for them to lose sight of him. There was only one option, I spoke to Petrov and explained the problem. He saw the solution instantly.

"Certainly, Jurgen, you want me to leave a nice present for our friends."

"I do, but there's no time for anything sophisticated. Can you do something on the run, without stopping to prepare?"

He thought for a moment.

"A remote detonation, the communists' favourite method. I'll prepare a charge, if you would take the wire and move fifty metres into the jungle while I'm hiding it. Find some cover, as soon as it's ready I'll join you. When our friends reach the charge, just trigger it. I'll keep an eye out for a good spot."

"Fine, I'll send Schuster back to let Bauer and Fassbinder know what we're doing."

We kept running, within half a kilometre we found the right place, where the track narrowed and would funnel the Viets into a tight group. Petrov had prepared a rough and ready charge, he stopped and began to bury it in a tangle of foliage. I hurtled into the jungle, laying out the cable as I ran, after about fifty metres I found a fallen tree trunk which made good enough cover. I saw Bauer, Schuster and Fassbinder run past, then Petrov came scrambling through the undergrowth to join me behind the tree trunk. Within minutes, we heard the sound of the pursuit, the Viets were keeping up the fast pace, their equipment rattling as they ran gave them away. I saw them come into view, a group of about ten. They were bunched up, not expecting any kind of an ambush. I let them come abreast of the charge, then pressed the switch on the detonator. There was a blinding flash, the crash of the explosion and a massive shock wave surged through the jungle and battered everything around us. Leaves and greenery were tossed high into the air, mixing with smoke and dust to obliterate our view of the blast site.

As the dust began to settle, I heard firing, then the rest of our men came into view, hitting the surviving Viets hard before they had time to recover. They poured a withering fire on the survivors, it was no contest. In less than half a minute, the Viets were all dead. I noticed Helene standing next to a tree where she'd been sheltering from the gunfire. She came over to look at the bodies, but they were beyond her help. She shook her head despairingly, then crossed herself and said a silent prayer.

"We need to get moving," I shouted, "we've only won ourselves a small lead on the enemy. They'll know the direction we're headed in, so if we don't keep moving they'll be back on our tails again soon. Move out."

We continued our dash though the jungle, following the track that Pham had shown us when she brought us in. We approached Dong Khe carefully, but there was no sign of any increased activity. We pushed on, skirting the town and continued heading south.

Every hour I stopped them for a short break, but time was not on our side. We pushed on late into the night, until it was so dark we couldn't even follow the track. I ordered a stop and we made camp.

Giap had managed to keep up, he was much fitter than I would have imagined most army commanders would be. Perhaps it was his life organising and controlling a guerrilla army that kept him in shape. He spent every day undercover, moving from place to place, in fear of discovery by the French. Now his worst fears were realised. I made sure that he was secured for the night, two troopers were assigned to watch him. His hands were still tied, in addition I made them link his bound hands to a tree, so that escape was all but impossible.

During the night, we heard the sound of engines moving down the main track that led from Dong Khe. There was the unmistakable equipment rattle of troops moving, the urgent commands of officers and the sounds of the beginnings of a huge search operation. The Viets could call on several divisions to scour the countryside, I wondered if one hostage, even one so prominent as Giap, would be enough to keep us alive.

CHAPTER EIGHT

In the morning we ate a hasty breakfast and prepared to move out. There was no question of using the direct route south, the whole area was crawling with Viet Minh troops searching for Giap, I called the men for a meeting to discuss our options.

"We are here, about thirty kilometres south of Dong Khe," I said, pointing to a spot on the map. "Here's the prison camp we visited on the way in, here's the plantation. The main track is obviously out of the question, as far as I can see, the only alternative is to travel through the swamps."

They groaned, the Indochinese swamps were notorious. The hazards were endless, malaria mosquitoes, snakes, poisonous insects and constant flies that made life an unending hell. Then of course there were the leeches. Even the locals avoided the swamps and there were many tales, some probably apocryphal, of groups of people entering the swamps never to be seen again.

"I know, I know, but we don't have a choice. It's the swamps or Giap's people, and they'll be a damn sight nastier than the swamps. Let's get moving."

We picked up our packs and weapons and moved east. Would the Viets work out where we were? Certainly they would consider that we'd tried for the swamps, but finding us there would be another matter.

They could search for us with ten divisions of troops before they got on our trail. Then again, they probably would search for us with ten divisions of troops. It was a sobering thought.

We travelled for five kilometres before we reached the edge of the swamps. Then the going became really hard, before long we were wading through waist deep water. We all kept a look out for snakes and any other nasty creatures that could be a threat, but really there was little we could do other than hope that the passage of a large group of people would be enough to make them keep well away.

We kept water out of our gun barrels by using condoms stretched over the end. Petrov carried his pack of explosives on top of his head, careful to keep it well away from the water. As usual we used a point and rear guard formation. This time Schuster went with Armand to check the route through the damp, green hell. Schuster had found a long sapling, broken out of the ground, which he used to probe in front of him, checking that the water did not unexpectedly become too deep.

I estimated we were making barely a kilometre an hour. At this rate, it would be several days before we even managed to escape the main search area and move back onto a jungle track that would enable us to push a faster pace. At one rest stop I talked to Bauer and Schuster about the supply situation.

"Jurgen, we have supplies for another day, no more. We can't hang around here for too long, even assuming that the men don't begin to fall ill." Schuster had checked every pack and inventoried the supplies of food, we were running dangerously low. We'd planned the mission on the basis of being able to replenish food supplies from local villages. The problem was that there were no villages in the swamps.

I checked the map.

"Very well, we need to head slightly north, I know, it's taking us in the wrong direction. But it will confuse the Viets and more importantly, take us out of the swamps."

We checked out the map thoroughly, but it was the only sensible alternative. Staying in the swamp much longer and hunger and illness would be certain to hit us, sooner rather than later. I needed to lead a fighting force back to Hanoi, not a troop of the halt and the lame.

I told the men what we were planning, which cheered them up. The effect of the swamp was depressing, a constant wait to see what would strike first, snakes, leeches, or the deadly bouts of malarial attack that reduced men to quivering invalids. By the early evening we were getting to higher ground, and soon we were out of the swamp and able to make camp on dry ground.

We slumped down, exhausted and I went to check on Giap. His hands were still tied, and I carefully untied them so that he could revive the circulation in his arms. He flexed his muscles with some relief.

"Thank you, Sergeant," he said.

"I don't think you have anywhere to run, Comrade Giap."

"Do you think you'll ever get me to Hanoi?" he asked.

I looked him in the eyes, and he stared back.

"I think we both know that getting you to Hanoi is not much of an option, Giap. There are about ten of your divisions searching for you, we'll be lucky to get halfway.

"So what do you plan to do with me? Shoot me, is that it? I know that you never intended to give me back to my men. That was just a way for you to escape."

I nodded. "Yes, that's true. Wouldn't you have done the same thing?"

"Of course, this is a war. A guerrilla war without rules, like the Chinese fought against Chiang Kai Chek, Lenin's revolution in Russia, even your French Revolution."

"I am not French."

"Where do you come from, then?"

"I am German, what your people might call a Nazi."

"German?" He looked at me with new interest. "So you fought in the Great Patriotic War?"

I smiled. The Russians had given it that name, we just called it the Eastern Front.

"Yes, I fought in Russia."

"And lost in Russia, Sergeant. You found the Russians more than a match, did you not?"

"We certainly lost," I agreed.

"But no, not because the Russians were better fighters. They were tough yes, they often fought on when lesser men would have given up. But man for man we gave them a hammering. We were beaten by politics, my friend, politics in the shape of a madman who was in charge."

"Hitler," he said. "The greatest war criminal the world has ever known."

I laughed. "He was certainly bad, but Comrade Stalin was far worse."

"Stalin?" he said abruptly. "Stalin was a hero, a great leader of the people."

"He was a butchering war criminal," I told him. "Ready to butcher his own people. Men, women and children, if it might help the war effort. Sometimes just because he felt like it."

He shook his head in disbelief.

"Comrade Stalin saved a whole nation from defeat at the hands of your leader, Hitler. He was one of the greatest men who ever lived."

I was intrigued to hear him defending Stalin. Giap was an educated man, very, very clever. He knew very well how evil Stalin had been, certainly the equal of Hitler in bloodletting. Or did he?

I wondered just how much he did know and how much was just the party line that he fed to poor peasants. The peasants who hoped that following the communists would give them freedom, land, food, a job, all the things that made people's lives bearable the world over. All of the things that once they gained power the communists turned their backs on.

I told him what I'd seen in Russia, of Stalin's NKVD and commissars ordering civilians to walk over minefields to clear the way for their troops. Of women and children shot for fleeing embattled cities, even when as civilians they were just trying to save their lives when Stalin had failed them. Of the Gulags, of the 'Stalin Terror' purges of the late 1930's.

"Well of course some things are necessary. Revolution is a messy business, sometimes it is necessary to lose a few lives in the process of building a new and great nation." Giap said.

"Women, children, the old and sick, the wounded and disabled?" I said, appalled.

"Of course. They're all part of the revolution, no one has the right to stand idly by while someone fights for their freedom."

"Freedom?" I laughed. "The people of Russia are anything but free. They're just inmates in Stalin's great prison camp. Or do you mean freedom for the members of the Politburo, for people like yourself?"

He looked angry, but I knew I'd hit a nerve. Giap was not used to arguing against someone who had seen the outside world, had seen what communism had done to an entire nation, enslaved it, turned whole countries into police states.

"Before Stalin," he retorted angrily, "the Russian peasant was just a slave of the landowner. Most spent their entire lives in total, abject poverty, fighting each day to just get enough to eat."

I nodded. "You're right, the Russian Tsars, the aristocracy, treated them like chattels, slaves to buy and sell, to spend their entire lives working for the benefit of the rich. But the communists were not the answer. They gave the peasants a few benefits, some were able to get enough to eat, somewhere to live. Many did not, you know about the famines, the mass killings, the forced emigrations? Sure, Russia was a hell for the peasants before the communists, but it's still a hell. I know you won't believe it, but I can assure you that many of them greeted the German armies with garlands of flowers when we invaded. They were happy to accept anything that would remove them from the enslavement of communism."

"So why did they fight so hard to beat the Germans?" he asked.

"They fought for a lot of reasons. Because they were ordered to and they were threatened with being shot if they didn't. And Hitler stupidly decreed that they should be treated as 'untermensch', sub-humans, so that they quickly learned to hate us. If we'd treated the Russians as allies instead of killing and enslaving them, we could have beaten Stalin in a month."

He was thoughtful after that. Obviously he was already aware of the worst of Stalin's excesses, his murderous rule over the Soviet Union after the death of Lenin. But somehow I thought that he was still trying to fit this new knowledge of the war into his scheming, into his political philosophy, so that he could twist it to his advantage.

I left him then and went back to join the others. Corporal Dubois and Private Laurent were guarding Giap, with orders to kill him if he made any attempt to escape. Helene was waiting for me.

"You've been talking to Giap?" she asked me.

"That's right," I replied.

"Did you get anything out of him?"

I suddenly realised that she thought I'd been interrogating him, probably torturing him. Women!

"I gagged him and then sliced all his fingers off, the way the Gestapo showed me," I replied.

"One at a time."

Her eyes widened.

"My God, that is terrible, you're, a ..." she tried to think of the worst thing possible. "You're an animal. You disgust me."

I smiled, and then couldn't resist laughing.

"What are you laughing about?" she asked.

Then realisation hit her.

"You're pulling my leg! Jurgen, you swine," she began laughing too.

"I didn't believe you, you know."

"I'm not too sure about that," I grinned.

"For one moment, I thought you were about to have my men arrest me for war crimes."

"I still might," she pouted. "What are you going to do about him? Giap, I mean. How can you get him back to Hanoi when most of the Viet Minh are scouring the country for him?"

"I don't know, Helene. You're right, getting him back would be impossible. At the start of the mission we were getting help from the Navy, the plan was that they would send a helicopter to take him away, then we were to head for the coast and pick up a ride on a Naval destroyer."

"So why can't you do that?"

"Politics, my dear. Certain people wouldn't allow it, who knows what pressures were brought to bear? But the end result was that we were left on our own."

"So what will you do with him?"

I didn't answer.

We sat for a while longer, just enjoying each other's company. Then we turned in to get a night's sleep, away from the festering flies and insects of the swamp. I checked the sentry roster, then lay down and promptly fell asleep. I woke quickly, grabbing for my pistol, but a finger was pushed against my lips.

"Schh," Helene said.

She was crouched over me, with a blanket wrapped around her. She crawled under my own blanket and pulled her own off, she was naked. I felt myself becoming aroused at the unusual and totally unexpected prospect of having a beautiful, naked young woman in bed with me in the midst of the Indochinese jungle with Ho Chi Minh's hordes hunting us down like dogs. She kissed me, a long, lingering, passionate kiss that sent a tingle through my whole body.

"Don't say anything, please, Jurgen. Just love me," she whispered.

So I did, I caressed her body, kissed her all over, felt the warm, smooth curves, her delicious breasts, smelled the overpowering scent of woman on her, exaggerated by the long, hot day we had spent fleeing from the Viets. I felt between her legs, where she was already wet, her body arching up inviting me to join her. I pulled down my trousers I always slept in when in the field, already my organ was rock hard, ready to enter her. She pulled me towards her and we made passionate love. Not only the hot sex of two souls thousands of miles from home and desperate for the warmth of human contact, the most basic and primeval form of human contact, but I felt more, and was sure that she did too. The sex was wonderful, though conducted in as muted and discrete a fashion as possible. The last thing we needed was for the whole camp to know that we had become lovers. Then I fell asleep again, when I was roughly awakened by the sentry. She had already gone back to her own bedroll.

It wasn't quite dawn. The whole camp was coming to. I quickly pulled on my jacket and equipment, picked up my submachine gun and went to find Giap. Helene noticed my going, I could tell by the way she looked, the fear and sadness in her eyes, that she understood that her lover of the night before was about to become an executioner. I ignored her and approached Giap, still fastened to a tree out of sight of the camp and guarded by two of the men. I told them to leave, then spoke to Giap. He knew what was coming, but as far as I could tell, was not afraid.

"So, Sergeant. You have come to kill me?"

"Wouldn't you, Giap, if you were in my place?"

"Probably, if it was necessary, yes, I would kill you. Or me, as it happens," he acknowledged.

I got out my knife, a sharpened combat knife. For the first time he showed fear but quickly got himself under control. I reached behind him and cut his bonds, freeing his arms.

"I am releasing you, Comrade Giap, unharmed. You can go back to your people."

He was stunned.

"Why?"

"Why not?" I said to him. "I'm a soldier, not an assassin. If the High Command wants you dead, they can come and do it themselves."

"The SS were famous for killing their prisoners, were they not?" he said, perplexed.

"Some were, yes, but most of us didn't kill prisoners. We didn't treat them well either, but we weren't murderers. We were German soldiers, the best in the world, my friend, no more, no less. Now, get going before I change my mind."

I gave him a bottle of water.

"That will have to be enough, I'm afraid."

"So what was it all for, Sergeant? Why did you come on the mission in the first place?"

"I honestly don't know," I said, surprising myself in the realisation that I really didn't know. "Perhaps it was like climbing a mountain, because it was there. Perhaps at the time it seemed the right thing to do."

"Very well, Sergeant. It is ironic, is it not, that if you had arrived two days later, we would have taken you?"

I raised my eyebrows. "You think so?"

"Of course," he smiled, "we were preparing a suitable welcome for you…" he trailed off.

"You were saying?" I said curtly.

"Nothing," he replied. "Now I will leave."

He held out his hand. "Until we meet again, Sergeant."

I shook his hand. "If I meet you in battle, I'll kill you."

He smiled. "No doubt. I don't suppose you would consider joining me? I could offer you a senior command."

"Change sides? Absolutely not."

He shrugged. "Then I wish you a safe journey back. Goodbye, Sergeant."

He set out on the path back to Cao Bang, walking calmly away from me. A man who knew where his fate would lead him. I wondered what he'd meant by preparing a welcome for us. It seemed we had a traitor in Hanoi, that was something to be investigated. I turned and went back to the men, who erupted when I told them what I'd done.

"Jurgen, for God's sake, all this effort, for nothing. Why the hell did you do it?"

Karl-Heinz Vogelmann glared at me, his face red with anger. The rest of them were no happier. It was time to explain the tactical realities

"Look men, here is the situation. As long as we had Giap, there would be upwards of ten thousand hostile Viet Minh hunting us down. There are twelve of us, and we still have a hundred and fifty kilometres to travel to get back to Hanoi. We're in the middle of Viet held territory, our only hope is to call off the hunt. How long do you think we would last with that many Viet Minh soldiers hunting us? Let alone the civilians, who would all have been alerted to keep watch. Our own High Command has told us that they will not send in air support, or any other support, for fear of upsetting the Americans. Giap will be back with his people within hours, you know how communications work in the jungle, that means the heat will be off. It was a simple choice, keep Giap and we were looking at fighting off thousands of Viet Minh, an impossibility. There is no question we all would have died. I had to release him to give us a chance of getting back to Hanoi."

"There was another choice, Jurgen."

"Really," I replied to Vogelmann, still red faced and angry. "What was that?"

"Kill him, finish the bastard off."

I nodded.

"That was an option, of course. Two problems there, Karl-Heinz. Firstly, how would that take off the pressure of the Viet Minh searching for him and eventually getting into a firefight with us that we couldn't win?"

He was silent.

"The second problem is this. Who was going to kill him, who is the executioner? You, Karl-Heinz? Is that what you're fighting for, to execute a brave man who has only ever done his duty? You want us to turn into an Einsatzgruppe?"

He looked way, embarrassed.

The Einsatzgruppen were our SS paramilitary death squads, responsible for mass killings, of Jews in particular, but also significant numbers of other population groups and political categories in the countries overrun by the German armed forces. The Einsatzgruppen followed the German invasions of Poland, in September, 1939, and later, of the Soviet Union in June 1941. Einsatzgruppen carried out operations ranging from the murder of a few people to those which lasted over two or more days, such as the massacres at Babi Yar where 33,471 were killed in two days and Rumbula, where 25,000 died in two days.

The Einsatzgruppens were responsible for the murders of over a million people, and they were the first Nazi organisations to commence mass killing of Jews as an organised policy. Their activities sickened both Waffen-SS and regular army alike. Many of their members were recruited from occupied countries, Lithuania, the Ukraine and Latvia amongst others.

None of us had ever served in such a unit, but their methods were well known and despised by the rest of the army.

There was a visible relaxing of the tension as they realised that despite the impossible dilemma we had been in, we had not chosen to become outright murderers.

"Look, it was a good try, but I now realise that when the High Command refused any help we were dead in the water. Maybe we shouldn't have come, but it's too late to worry about that now. Besides, the prisoners we released in that camp were worth the trip, as well as Helene and the villagers, so we've hit the Viets pretty hard. What we need to do is move away from this area, because as soon as Giap is picked up, he'll send them here to hunt for us. We'll move south east, away from Hanoi, and cut back to the west when things have gone quiet."

"How long do you estimate they'll keep searching for us," Bauer asked.

"I'd give them twelve hours maximum to locate Giap, Friedrich, at least a couple of days before the search scales down, so we need to lay low for about three days. Let's get moving now, we'll find somewhere to make camp and sit it out."

"I'll get them moving, then," he replied.

He began giving orders and the men picked up their weapons and packs ready to move out. Within minutes we were once more picking our way through the jungle, this time moving at a tangent from our original direction to throw off the enemy.

We travelled all day, twice stopping when we heard large numbers of Viet Minh troops moving nearby. It was obvious the search was still going on, as I expected. We would need to hide deep in the jungle to stay hidden. By the evening we'd found the perfect place. Kessler had stopped to relieve himself, moving off the path to spare Helene's blushes. He came back out grinning.

"Ok, you lot, I've found where can make camp, come and take a look."

We followed him through a narrow gap between two trees, almost invisible from the path. We found ourselves in a narrow tunnel, surrounded by thick foliage. This ran for three or four metres, then opened up into a natural clearing, with of all things a small stream running along one side.

"I've checked the water, it's fresh and clear, no natives pissing in it upstream."

"You're right, Manfred, this will be perfect. We'll make camp here for three days and then we can get back on our return journey to Hanoi."

I called over to Sergeant Schuster.

"Paul, take a couple of men and check the trail, make sure that you cover our traces. It might be worth laying a false trail, about a kilometre or so past this place, in case the Viet trackers get onto us."

"I'll get right on it, Jurgen," he said, calling to Nikolai Petrov and Private Armand.

Petrov especially was a master of disguise, a skill he'd perfected when laying his various charges and booby traps.

The rest of us threw off our packs, put down our weapons, and gratefully filled up our water bottles from the stream. The water was delicious, cold and clear, there was indeed no sign of any 'native piss' in it. I posted sentries on the entrance to the clearing, their orders were simple, keep totally silent and report any movement nearby.

Then I went to find a good spot to rest, it had been a tense, hard day's hike through the jungle, with the constant threat of Giap's men hitting us with an ambush. Several of the men were covered in sores, others had bites. I took off my jacket and shirt, my arms were covered in red blotches and jungle sores, a result of salt in my perspiration and bites from innumerable insects. Helene came up to me.

"Jurgen, that looks bad, allow me to fix you up."

I waited gratefully while she delved into her pack and got out a tube of salve, which she began daubing over my skin. It was cool and soothing, even more so perhaps because of the beautiful young woman who was applying it, it was a very arousing experience. If she noticed the lump in my trousers, she tactfully avoided mentioning it. Finally, she applied some bandages to the worst affected places. It felt wonderful and I thanked her.

"You're welcome Jurgen. I must leave you now, I need to check the other men. I'll be back when I've finished."

She moved off, the men visibly brightened as she reached each of them and checked them over. It took her almost an hour to patch everyone up, then she came back and we shared some of the cold rations. There would be no more hot food until we got back into friendly territory, the smell of a fire would bring Viet Minh from miles around.

"Tell me, Jurgen," she said, as we sat comfortably spooning down some sort of a stew out of tin cans. "Why didn't you kill Giap?"

"I thought I made it clear, it wouldn't have helped us. The Viets would have kept looking."

"Would you have killed him, if they ordered you too?" she persisted.

"Those were my orders, in fact, to bring him back if possible, to kill him if it wasn't."

"You disobeyed an order?" She was astonished.

"Of course. You thought I'd commit murder?"

"If you were ordered to, yes, I honestly thought you would. But I'm pleased you didn't," she added.

"It seems the reputation of the SS killers is hard to shake off," I said ruefully.

"Listen, Helene, I'm a soldier. That means I sometimes have to kill people, usually when they are trying to kill me. Occasionally, I kill civilians when they are unfortunate enough to get caught in cross fire. But murdering a man in cold blood is not something I've ever done, nor contemplated. Oh sure, it went on in Russia, I saw it happen many times. On more than one occasion I have made my feelings known to a senior officer. So murder, no, it's not my style."

She smiled. "I apologise, I have misjudged you."

I smiled back at her.

"In any case, killing Giap wouldn't have called off the hunt for him, would it?"

She leaned over and punched me on the arm.

"Damn you, Jurgen, just when I think you're a nice person you go and ruin it. What am I to make of you?"

"Whatever you want, my dear. What would you like to make of me?"

She looked me directly in the eyes. "Is that an invitation?"

"Absolutely, Helene, an open invitation. Shall we say tonight, and you can make of me as you will."

"Tonight, then," she said with a serious look on her face.

"Seriously, Jurgen, this war looks as if it will drag on forever. Do you see any future for us, for you and me?"

"I would like that, Helene, yes, I think I would. We're a long way from Hanoi, I think we have much to discuss when we get back."

"I would like that too," she replied.

We both sat silently, reflecting on what had just been said, and unsaid. Could I, formerly an SS officer, veteran of the Russian Front, Foreign Legion soldier and scourge of the Viet Minh, ever settle down to married life? With all the baggage that it carried with it, a home, children maybe, a regular job that didn't mean people shooting at you and you shooting at them? I realised then that yes, I could look forward to life with this beautiful, brave, fascinating woman. My God, how I was changing.

Helene came to me that night. I'd made my bed in the remotest part of the clearing. She said that she hoped no one would notice. I didn't tell her that in a tight unit like this one they noticed everything. You couldn't even sneeze without half the men finding it amusing.

We made love, silently, passionately, the bond between us even stronger now that we both knew that this relationship planned to become permanent. If we got back to Hanoi, of course. She was naked underneath my blanket, her skin smooth and elastic. The smell of her, the musky smell of a fit young woman, even more prominent after the hot, sweaty forced march through the jungle, was especially arousing. That evening, I knew in my mind that this was the woman for me, the one I wanted to be my mate for the rest of my life. Once again, in the morning she was gone. We spent three days in that jungle clearing, three glorious days in which we relaxed, re-cuperated and generally got ourselves back to fitness, whilst the Viet Minh hunt died down. Each day, there were alarms as the sentries ran into the clearing to report the approach of a group of men. We kept still and quiet while they went past, we were not using anything that they could smell, like soap, toothpaste, aftershave, any of the things that beginners to jungle warfare gave themselves away with.

We were one with the jungle, no unfamiliar noise or smells, just an isolated universe, of no threat to the armed groups, nor them to us, as long as we remained undiscovered.

After the three days the numbers of passing hunters had almost dropped to zero. It was time to move, I gave the orders, we picked up our packs and weapons and left our jungle haven. We travelled as usual with two scouts well to the front, as well as two men in the rear to watch for any unexpected pursuit. It took us six days to get back to Hanoi, six days of hacking and slashing our way through isolated, often abandoned jungle trails.

Despite my freeing Giap, I knew that he would not let up until he had exhausted every possibility to capture and if neces-sary wipe out my group, which had come so close to upsetting the communist plans in Indochina. So we carefully avoided any tracks or trails that looked well used. It was hard going, blaz-ing trails where probably no human being had passed in several years. The paths were overgrown with bushes and vines. Often, the trails themselves became impossible to identify and we had to navigate by compass.

But our caution paid off, in six days we only came close to enemy contact twice, and on both occasions we had sufficient warning from our scouts to give us time to get into cover. On the evening of the sixth day, we came out onto a French military road, and in less than an hour had hitched a lift on an empty supply lorry returning to Hanoi after supplying one of the outlying forts. Just before dark we drove through the barracks gates. We were home.

CHAPTER NINE

I reported in, found quarters for Helene and went back to my own room where I did my best to shower off the sweat and filth. I opened a bottle of Schnapps, drank a half of it and fell into bed, exhausted as the stress and tension of the mission drained out of me. I awoke suddenly to a knock on the door. Friedrich Bauer stood there.

"Its Joffre, Jurgen, he wants to speak with the Sergeants. Petrov and Schuster are already there, we need to report as soon as possible."

"He knows, Friedrich? About Giap?"

He nodded. "The word's got around that we had Giap and you let him go. My guess is he's not too happy."

"Ok, thanks Friedrich. I'll be there in twenty minutes, I need time for another shower."

"What will you tell him?" he asked.

"Tell Joffre? Fuck Joffre, I really don't give a damn. If he wants to murder Giap, he can go and do it himself. I'll see you there shortly," I said, dismissing him.

It was thirty minutes before I reported to Joffre, feeling belligerent and annoyed. Without doubt he could see it in my face. I lined up with Schuster, Bauer and Petrov in front of his desk.

"Sergeant Hoffman," he greeted me, "I will ask you later for a full report on the mission. In the meantime, I am disturbed at the suggestion that you had Giap and let him go. Is that correct?"

"Yes, Colonel, that is correct."

"I see," he responded heavily. "Would you tell me why you did it?"

I explained about the impossibility of returning safely to Hanoi through enemy territory with ten divisions of Viet Minh hunting us down.

"Very well, I understand all of that. Yes, you are quite correct, we already knew that the Viets threw a ring of troops around the approaches to Hanoi, even if you had escaped the immediate area they would have blocked your return. I imagine you anticipated that?"

"Yes, Sir," I replied.

"And the other option?"

"You mean murder, Colonel Joffre?"

He flinched.

"This is war, Sergeant Hoffman. There is a thin line between what we are forced to do and murder."

"Colonel, if we'd killed Giap, that wouldn't have called off the Viets. They would have kept hunting us."

"Yes, of course. So that is why you released him?"

"No, Colonel. I released him because I was never an executioner for the SS, neither will I become one for the French Foreign Legion."

He paused for a moment, his expression was angry.

"Sergeant, by letting Giap go, you have made a grave mistake. I must report this to my superiors."

I felt my anger boil over.

"Colonel, I suggest you report it to the same superiors who were too cowardly to offer us the support we needed. If they had had the guts to send in helicopters for an air evacuation, we could have been back here a week ago, complete with Comrade Giap. As it is, I wasn't prepared to be a murderer, nor to be party to the effective murder of my men, which would have happened if we hadn't released him. Now if you want my sergeant's stripes, you can have them. And if you want me to resign from the Legion, you can have that too. Sir!" I shouted.

The others looked at me, astonished. I was not always the most obedient of soldiers, but I rarely lost my temper, and never with a senior officer. I saluted, turned on my heel and stormed out of the office.

An hour later the sergeants came to my room.

"Well," I asked them, "who is to take over the unit?"

"You're still in charge, Jurgen. Now that Joffre has the full facts, he can see your point of view. On top of that, the senior officer that we released from the prison camp has just been on the phone, he wants to recommend you for a medal. When he put the phone down, Helene came to the office and told him her side of the story, about the freeing of those villagers. Putting it all together, we scored pretty well, even returning without Giap. We certainly had more success against the Viets than the whole of the French Army has had in the past year." Petrov said.

"Helene? Where is she now?" I asked them.

"She's gone to report to the Medical Administrator for Indochina, the guy who runs the charity she works for. She'll be back some time this afternoon," Bauer said.

"Thanks, Friedrich. In that case, as I'm still in charge, I've got something to do. Before I let him go, Giap let slip that someone fed the Viets information about our mission."

"That would explain a lot, there were far too many Viets in the area, many more than we expected."

"So who was it? Anyone got any ideas about who ratted us out?"

They shook their heads.

I told them of my suspicions, of my chats with the men on the way back, especially with Manfred von Kessler.

Von Kessler had been seeing a Viet girl for some time. I'd had my suspicions aroused when I caught her one day outside the room where we were discussing our forthcoming mission.

"It would be best to speak to Manfred," Paul Schuster said. "Thien is a sweet girl, I've met her on several occasions when she has been here with Manfred. But if there is any question about her being a spy, well…"

He tailed off. Well indeed, if Manfred's girl was a spy, she would need to be dealt with.

"I'll go and find him now and have a chat. Friedrich, Joffre is waiting for the mission report, would you do me a favour and make a start. I have a feeling that this business with Thien won't wait."

"Ok, Jurgen, no problem."

I left the room and went to find Manfred. He was in the armoury, supervising the checking and refitting of our heavy weapons. Von Kessler was a dedicated soldier that was obvious. In this war, it paid to always be ready for the next mission, no matter how recently the last one had finished.

"Manfred, I need a word," I greeted him.

"Jurgen, you look serious. A problem?"

"Let's go outside for a chat."

We found the canteen empty and sat down with a couple of cold beers.

"It's about Thien," I told him.

"What about her? Has she done anything wrong?"

I went over the various scraps of information we'd gathered together, the listening at doors, the hint that Giap had dropped, as well as other suspicions that had surfaced over the past few weeks.

"Taken one by one these reports could be ignored, but together, they all point to Thien being involved with the Viets, Manfred."

He had gone red in the face. I hadn't realised how close he was to the girl.

"Jurgen, I'd stake my life on Thien being clean. Damnit, anyone could be a spy. What about Mai?"

Mai was Karl-Heinz Vogelmann's girlfriend. I had to agree that it was also possible, although less likely. She didn't hang around the barracks like Thien, and seemed less likely a candidate.

"Look, we need to get the girls in for questioning, Manfred. Just a friendly chat, no rough stuff, perhaps they are both innocent. Would you find Karl-Heinz and both of you go and find your girlfriends and bring them back here?"

"I'll get onto it right away. The sooner we can clear this up the better. I'll let you know when we get back with the girls."

We finished our beers and he walked away to find Vogelmann and locate the girls. An hour later, they both came back, red-faced.

"They've gone, Jurgen."

"Gone? Both of them?"

"We checked everywhere, their homes, the bars, the usual places. Thien's mother said that she hasn't been home for two days, Mai's parents said that she hasn't been home either," von Kessler said hurriedly.

"Maybe they were both up to something, perhaps they got word from the Viets that we might suspect them." I said.

"Or perhaps they refused to help the Viets and were kidnapped, at this stage we don't know anything until we can locate them," Vogelmann added.

"Either way, we need to find out what has happened to them. Jurgen, we could do with some help to start searching," said von Kessler.

"Of course. It's a security matter now, not just a couple of lost girlfriends, so I'll clear it with Joffre. I think six of us should do it. Hopefully there'll be a simple explanation and we can put this behind us," I replied.

In the event, Joffre needed no convincing.

"I'm concerned that you all need a rest after that last mission, Jurgen, but I do agree that finding out if these girls are a security leak is a priority concern."

I thanked him and left. We spent the rest of the afternoon hunting for the girls, questioning the locals and checking every known haunt where they might be holed up. We came up with nothing, and as afternoon turned into evening found a bar that offered decent food and sat down for a meal and to discuss our strategy. The waitress brought out steaming plates of Banh Chung, sticky rice wrapped in banana leaves and stuffed with mung bean paste, lean pork and black pepper together with fresh glasses of ice cold beer. We were wolfing down the food, the first really good meal we'd eaten in a long time, when Petrov suddenly leapt out of his seat, picked up his MP40 submachine gun and dashed out of the restaurant. We heard the sounds of a struggle, raised voices, shouting, screams of pain, then a massive explosion. We dived to the floor and crawled over to the window, all of us had our weapons out and ready to fire. Nikolai was standing over the prostrate form of a Viet. Near-by, the explosion had smashed apart a palm tree, which had crashed to the ground, riddled with metal fragments. There was no obvious threat, so we cautiously left the restaurant and went over to Petrov.

"Sorry about the fuss, Jurgen. I saw this bastard," he indicated the body of the Viet on the ground with a kick, "sneaking past with something in his hand. I thought it might be a grenade, so I rushed out and grabbed him. He'd already pulled out the pin, so I had to chuck it somewhere safe. Pity about the tree," he said ruefully.

"What about him?" I asked, nodding towards the body on

the ground.

"Knocked out, I hit him pretty hard, I think." He grinned.

I turned over the body. The man was still breathing, looked to be a typical northern Viet, I guessed his age at about twenty. He was well dressed, not one of the usual peasants who mounted isolated and sporadic attacks on us at the command of their Viet Minh slave masters. This one looked like a student, possibly from Hanoi University. He began groaning, then looked up at his captors. There was strangely no fear in his eyes, just hatred, vicious and intense.

"Now, my friend, who are you?" I asked him.

He just stared so I repeated the question. There was still no response.

"We'll take him back to the barracks, we need to question him. Maybe he can throw some light on the whereabouts of Thien and Mai."

As I said the names, I saw his eyes react. Got you, you bastard, I thought. He definitely knew something about them, we just needed to get it out of him. We tied his hands with some twine that Petrov had in his pocket and marched our captive back to barracks. When we got there I sent for Corporal Dubois and Private Laurent, the two Arabs. They arrived within minutes. Bruno's eyes lit up when he saw the Viet trussed and ready for a 'talk'.

"Corporal, this prisoner tried to kill us with a hand grenade. I want him interrogated, especially with regards to the whereabouts of Thien and Mai, von Kessler and Vogelmann's girlfriends. They went missing a couple of days ago, I want to know why, and where they are at present. You have a free hand, so do whatever is necessary. But keep it quiet," I said, looking at him meaningfully.

"I don't want some bleeding heart in the barracks whining about torture and mistreating prisoners."

"Understood, Sergeant. I'll make sure he's as quiet as a sleeping baby." Dubois grinned.

"Report to me when you have something, and remember, whatever it takes, provided it makes no noise."

Dubois left with the prisoner. We went over to the canteen and I bought another round of beers to replace the ones we'd left in the restaurant when the grenade went off. We chatted quietly, waiting for Dubois to get results. Vogelmann and von Kessler especially were edgy, it was their girlfriends that may be in trouble. Either they were spying for the Viets, or they had been kidnapped for consorting with a French soldier. Either way, it meant trouble.

Two hours went by and I was about to go and ask Dubois about progress when he entered the canteen. He wore a broad smile on his face.

"We have the information you wanted, Sergeant. The man's name is Trinh Van Dung, he's a student at the University. In his spare time he works as an agent of the local Viet Minh cadre. The attack was his own idea. Apparently, he saw you in the bar and thought it would be easy to throw the grenade and get away."

"And the girls, any information on them?" I asked.

"He knows the names. He heard the local girls are girl-friends of two of our soldiers and that one of the girls was working for the Viets. The other one found out and was going to report it to us, but the Viets got to her first."

"Does he know which was which, who was informing?"

He shook his head.

"Sorry, no. I pressed him hard, but he doesn't know. He gave me an address where we can find them, though."

He handed me a scrap of paper with a local address written on it. It was a brothel in the Ba Vi District, a good place to hide out, and also to get information on French troop movements. I knew that some of our legionnaires were occasional visitors to that brothel.

I thanked Dubois, he'd done a good job. The prisoner would be handed over now to our intelligence people, who would perhaps extract more information from him. Some of our interrogators were good and not too fussy about human rights and Geneva conventions. Others were sticklers for the rules and unlikely to get even the time of day from an enemy prisoner. Then I headed for Joffre.

"The thing is, Sir, that I believe this brothel in Ba Vi District is almost certainly a Viet Minh operation. It's a perfect cover, they'll have the police bribed so as to keep away. They have somewhere they can lay low, get information from our troops through the whores, probably they'll have arms stashed there as well. I would suggest a full scale operation, clear the place out and finish off any Viets who are hiding out there."

Joffre eyed me sceptically. "And release these two girlfriends at the same time, I suppose?"

"Colonel," I replied. "One of the two is certainly a traitor, giving away information to the Viets. So yes, we'll get them out, but one of them has a lot of questions to answer. The other is undoubtedly innocent."

He thought for a moment.

"Show me on the map, Sergeant."

We went over to the large scale map on his office wall, showing Hanoi and the surrounding districts. Ba Vi was about eight kilometres outside the town, reached by a French made road that guaranteed plenty of trade for the brothel.

"Very well, I'll agree to it. We don't know what we're getting into, Sergeant Hoffman. I'm sending the whole company, call Captain Leforge, we'll need to get him briefed."

As I walked out of the office to find Leforge, he added.

"You'd better pass on my order to get the company prepared for action, I want them ready to go by two o'clock. We'll stage the raid for the early hours of the morning."

By one the company was assembled in full battle order on the main parade ground. We were deployed between five trucks, with Leforge and myself in a command jeep, an American made Willys. The two of us went along the line of vehicles, making last minute checks. Colonel Joffre was standing by our jeep when we finished, he shook hands with both of us.

"Good luck, my friends. In the last couple of hours we've been rechecking intelligence reports, it seems that the information you got from the prisoner was the last part of a jigsaw. The brothel at Ba Vi is without doubt a Viet Minh operation. Your brief is to destroy it utterly, with as many of the Viets as possible. Keep a lookout for any of our men, they may be inside," he smiled.

"As for the two women, we need them alive, one is possibly innocent, the other certainly guilty. We need to know which is which, and interrogate the guilty one."

We both nodded our acknowledgment, boarded the jeep and departed, with the heavily laden lorries following. We drove towards the outskirts of the city, turned onto the Ba Vi road, then ran headlong into a roadblock.

Bullets began smashing into the vehicles, there was the chatter of a heavy machine gun. The road was blocked with logs that had been dragged all the way across the road, preventing the passage of anything larger than a bicycle. Leforge was shouting orders.

"Abandon the vehicles, take cover in the trees. Get the machine guns working, start giving covering fire!"

We leapt out of the jeep and rolled into the side of the road, away from the muzzle flashes of the ambushers' guns. The troops in the other vehicles did the same, inside of a minute our veteran legionnaires had started returning fire. The MG42's belched out their torrent of death with the familiar sound of tearing cloth, caused by the high rate of fire. The troops poured in more fire from their submachine guns and rifles, so that the enemy fire was quickly overwhelmed by our own fusillade. Although their machine gun was still firing, making movement difficult for us without being cut down by the spray of bullets. Leforge was lying next to me, firing his MP40 in short bursts, he twisted around to speak to me.

"Sergeant, we need to take out that machine gun. Any suggestions? Can you do anything?"

"Yes, Captain, I'll get on to it."

I crawled over to where Petrov and several of our troopers were huddled, firing aimed bursts at the areas where the enemy muzzle flashes gave away their positions.

"Nikolai, the machine gun. Can you make up a charge to throw at it, a grenade won't be enough to penetrate their cover."

"Sure, I've got something that should do the trick."

He foraged in his backpack and came out with a charge the size of a house brick.

"This should do it, the timer is set for five seconds. Just flick the switch here," he pointed at the trigger.

"Then throw it and run. Who's going to deliver this little present?"

"I'll do it, Jurgen, give it to me." It was Vogelmann.

"Quite honestly I've had enough tonight, the bastards kidnapped my girlfriend, now this. It's time to hit them back."

Vogelmann had something of a reputation as a thrower. In the 1936 Olympics, basketball had been added for the first time. Although mostly the exclusive preserve of the Americans and Canadians, many children in Nazi Germany were sufficiently impressed to practice hard for the time when it became a national sport. The war had stopped any chance of that, but not before Vogelmann had become a formidable competitor. I didn't doubt his ability to throw accurately.

He took the charge and crawled away. I ordered the men to increase their rate of fire to cover him, then I crawled back to Leforge.

"Any moment now," I told him.

Vogelmann stood up in a position almost on top of the Viet machine gun. He threw the charge, but as he did so the brilliant flash of a grenade burst lit up the scene clearly. A dozen Viets must have seen him clearly and they quickly switched aim.

With a sick feeling I saw his body jerk as round after round from the enemy guns smashed into him, the whole scene lit by a further grenade flash and the muzzle flashes of the gunfire. He was flung to the ground, a broken, lifeless, bloody ruin where seconds before he had been one of the finest NCOs in the Legion.

He was one of the bravest and most successful officers of the Waffen-SS Das Reich Division, with service in Russia, Italy and France. It had all ended for him here, in the damp, steaming jungles of Indochina whilst we were on a mission to attack a whorehouse. But it was no time for sentiment, his courageous attack had silenced the Viet machine gun, leaving their ambush strategy in tatters. Captain Leforge blew his whistle and the company rose as one man and charged the enemy positions, firing on the run.

I ran towards the most recent muzzle flash I had seen and went into the jungle. I immediately came upon a huddle of Viets, four of them, crouched behind their rifles and firing into my men. I emptied my MP40 into them, saw them all fall, never to rise again, changed clips and ran on.

All along the Viet position our troopers were doing the same thing, a high speed rush into the enemy, submachine guns, rifles and pistols blazing their message of death. I overran another position, taking out two more Viets. All around me I could hear the cries of agony as men were ripped to shreds by the high intensity of gunfire. The Viets stood no chance.

By our quick action and Vogelmann's bravery, we had turned the tables, had turned a possible defeat into victory. As the guns fell silent we began taking a roll call of our men. It took nearly twenty minutes to get the final tally, during which sporadic shots rang out as Viet wounded were despatched. I was talking to Captain Leforge when a man rose up in front of us and took aim with his rifle. Both Leforge and I cut him down instantly with pistol and submachine gun fire. A legionnaire came up to us.

"I have the numbers for you, Sir. We lost six dead."

Leforge was quiet for a moment. It was a heavy tally, yet inevitable in this war of phantoms and shadows when a straightforward manoeuvre could turn instantly into a vicious firefight that cost the lives of countless numbers of our men.

"Thank you, private. What about the enemy?"

"We killed sixty seven of them, Sir. Some got away, probably no more than five of them, looking at the cartridge cases and other signs around where they were positioned."

"Very well."

He looked at me.

"Any ideas, Jurgen? They seemed to know we were coming, how the hell did they manage it?"

Since I saw the road block, I'd thought of nothing else. I thought I had the answer.

"I think that the whole thing was a set up, I'm sorry, Captain. I suspect that the Viet we caught with the hand grenade outside the bar was meant to be caught and then 'forced' to give information, sending us down this road. We just fell into it."

"And the brothel? You think it wasn't a Viet operation?"

"I suspect it was, Captain, but I very much doubt it is now. Even if they'd wiped us all out, once our people knew about it they would have pulled out. No, they've moved somewhere else."

"Agreed, but how do we find out where that somewhere else is?"

"We need to talk to the prisoner again, Sir. At least, Corporal Dubois needs to talk to him. A very serious talk, I would suggest."

"But the prisoner has been handed over to our intelligence people, there is no way they would hand a valuable prisoner back," Leforge mused.

"In that case, we'd better retrieve him. Might I suggest a jailbreak?"

It may come to that, Jurgen," he smiled.

"We'll head back to barracks, it's time to hit them where it hurts. We'll get that prisoner out, never fear. You can tell your Corporal Dubois that the gloves are off. I want to know where the Viets are hiding out. This time, we'll wipe the evil bastards off of the face of the earth."

I smiled at the deadly intensity with which Leforge said those words. In truth, he'd been badly shocked, one moment dashing to raid a Viet Minh stronghold, the next returning to barracks with six of his men dead.

One of the trucks was unroadworthy, we distributed the men and equipment amongst the remaining vehicles. Petrov set booby trapped charges to take out a few more of the enemy when they tried to strip it. Then we boarded and left for the road back. It was a sombre journey, knowing that in the back of one of the lorries there were the bodies of six of our comrades, but it did serve to give us the determination to finish off this particular nest of Viet Minh vipers once and for all.

We drove in silence, finally entering the barracks gate around three thirty. It was a sobering thought that less than two hours ago we had charged out with such optimism and enthusiasm. Joffre was waiting for us just inside the gate, alerted by the heavy firing which they'd heard clearly in the barracks. Leforge ordered the driver to stop and he got out and spoke to the Colonel. I went over to join them in time to hear Joffre speaking.

"I'm sorry, Captain, but I cannot order the release into your custody of that prisoner. It is outside of my jurisdiction."

"Colonel, excuse me," I said, interrupting.

"If you would just agree to turn a blind eye, we'll take care of the rest of it ourselves."

He looked at me.

"I couldn't agree to the use of violence against our own men, Sergeant."

"Absolutely not, Sir."

"So how will you manage it then?"

"I was thinking that the Viets might try and stage a rescue, Colonel. No violence, there will only be one sentry on duty at the cell block at this time of night. Threaten him to hand over the keys, take out the prisoner and perhaps leave the sentry tied up."

"I'll agree on condition that your weapons are not loaded. Captain, I would want your word on that."

"This is Sergeant Hoffmann's operation, Sir, but I will give you that assurance. No guns to be loaded." Leforge replied.

"In that case, there's nothing more to be said. Goodnight,

gentlemen."

"Good night, Sir."

We exchanged salutes and Joffre went off to his quarters.

"You'd better get on with it, Sergeant," Leforge said.

"It'll be light soon, you need to be in and out before then."

"Yes, Sir. I'll let you know when we have the prisoner."

I left him and went to find the men, who were unloading equipment from the lorries.

"I want von Kessler, Dubois and Laurent to report to me in the company office," I told Friedrich Bauer.

"Send them to me on the double. Don't unload any more from the lorries, we might be going out again tonight."

He smiled. "What's going on, Jurgen?"

"I'll tell you later, Friedrich. I have a mission to plan. Get those men to me now."

I went over to the office, found the key to the store room and rummaged around in there for items of Viet clothing. I heard the legionnaires enter the office and called out to them.

"You three, come in here and get dressed."

They came into the storeroom and stopped, open mouthed.

"Jurgen," von Kessler said, "what the hell is going on?"

"You three are going to rescue the Viet prisoner," I told him, "disguised as Viet Minh."

He smiled understanding.

"I like the sound of that, you two, let's get dressed."

Fifteen minutes later we were creeping along the outside wall of the cell block. The plan went without a hitch. I waited outside to cover them, while Dubois, looking like a Viet Minh guerrilla, threatened the guard and made him lay down his rifle.

They took his key, unlocked Trinh's cell and came out with the prisoner. They tied and gagged the guard and put him in the cell, locking him in. Then we left with Trinh. In the dark, he didn't realise that his rescuers were not Viet Minh. As we left the cell block, he smiled his relief, then his face fell as he caught sight of me.

"Good evening, Comrade Trinh, I'm sorry about the inconvenience, but we haven't yet joined the communists."

"What do you want?" He asked, nervously.

"Just a chat, my friend, just a little chat."

He looked around in panic as he recognised Dubois and opened his mouth to scream. The Algerian corporal clamped his hand over the man's mouth and punched hard on the side of his head. He went down like a sack of potatoes.

"You haven't injured him, Dubois? We need to interrogate him soon." I said.

"Just a tap, Sergeant, he'll be back with us in a few minutes," he smiled, "I've done this a few times, I know exactly how hard to hit."

Ten minutes later Trinh was in the company office, tied to a chair, his mouth firmly gagged.

"Comrade Trinh," I said to him quietly. "Your ambush failed, you know, but I lost six men."

I saw the smile in his eyes, it was almost enough for me to want to kill him there and then. But we needed him alive.

The torture was not pretty, nor was the sight of Dubois so obviously enjoying the horrific pain that he forced the prisoner to suffer. Within a quarter of an hour Trinh was a bloody mass of pain and blood, parts of his body literally shredded, even his eyelids had been cut away. But he told us what we wanted to know.

Twenty minutes later we were mounted in the lorries, most of them still bearing the scars, the dents and bullet holes of their recent action, heading out to the Viet hideout. It was located in the Dong Anh district, a rural area. The Viets had taken over a Buddhist temple and used it as their headquarters. The monks had been killed and the temple was now staffed by their own people masquerading as Buddhist priests. Trinh told us that the main headquarters was in a series of tunnels built underneath the eastern side of the temple, approached through a hidden trapdoor underneath a particularly ornate statue of Buddha.

I decided to take him with us. He couldn't be left for our intelligence people to find out what we'd done to him. He was a brave man, training to be a commissar in the new Indochina, he'd almost died before he gave out the information. But the violence was necessary. We had to have the information. We roared out of the barrack gates, this time confident that we had a real, live target to hit.

CHAPTER TEN

This time we were taking no chances. Leforge led the way as before in his Willys jeep. We'd replaced the destroyed truck and were back to our compliment of five vehicles, each with twenty men and equipment. The US built Willys was fitted with a Browning .30 calibre medium machine gun, the gunner hanging on grimly to the mount as the jeep swerved around the corners. I rode in the lead truck, alongside the driver and machine gunner. Our trucks, American made two and a half tonners known as the 'deuce and a half', had a hatch over the cab with its own machine gun mount. We had mounted our MG42's so we packed a great deal of firepower. The rear canvases were rolled halfway up, so that ten men could observe each side for any signs of the enemy. If we ran into an ambush this time we intended to meet it head on with French firepower. Or German firepower, as von Kessler jokingly reminded me on occasions.

It was true, much of our ordnance was former Wehrmacht

equipment that was confiscated when Germany surrendered in May 1945. Along with the MG42's, we carried MP40 and MP38 sub machineguns as well as KAR 98 rifles. Some of our Foreign Legion units even used the Kubelwagen jeeps, a variant of the Volkswagen car, but they were not as popular as the Willys, being only two-wheel drive and less reliable than their American counterpart.

The journey to Dong Anh took us twenty five minutes. We had already pre-planned our arrival, essentially drive up, shoot everything that moved and then begin to look around. It was a simple plan but one we had used effectively many times before. The problem with this kind of war was that there was no way of knowing who was on the enemy side. A simple shopkeeper could suddenly become a Viet Minh fighter, reporting military movements to their commanders. They could pick up a rifle or submachine gun and start blazing away at our troops. The next minute, they were an 'innocent non-combatant', difficult to spot and almost impossible to eradicate.

So we found the best method was to strike like lightning before the enemy had time to pass the warning down the line. Hit them hard with everything we had before they even had time to finish a meal. If was of course a variant of the 'Blitzkrieg' principle we Germans had used in the Second World War.

Blitzkrieg, or lightning war, was a term that described the force concentration of tanks, infantry, artillery and air power. Concentrating overwhelming force and rapid speed to break through enemy lines, and once the latter is broken, proceeding without regard to its flank. Through constant motion, the Blitzkrieg attempts to keep its enemy off balance, making it difficult to respond effectively at any given point before the front has already moved on.

When Germany invaded Poland in 1939, Western journalists had adopted the term Blitzkrieg to describe this form of armoured warfare. The operations were very effective during the early Blitzkrieg campaigns of 1939 to 1941. They were dependent on surprise penetrations, like the penetration of the Ardennes forest region, general enemy unpreparedness and an inability to react swiftly enough to the attacker's offensive operations. During the Battle of France, French attempts to re-form defensive lines along rivers were constantly frustrated when our German forces arrived there first and pressed on.

The gunner tapped me on the shoulder. He also served as the radio operator.

"Message from the Captain to all vehicles, contact in five minutes."

I acknowledged the message and signalled to the men in the back, they nodded their understanding. They had each prepared their own firing position, with boxes and kitbags piled into protective emplacements. They crouched in readiness, weapons cocked, grenades ready for instant use. The machine gunners constantly traversed around, checking for the smallest sign that would indicate an enemy target. Von Kessler was nearest to me in the back of the lorry, he leaned over to speak to me.

"Jurgen, I'm worried about Thien. If she's a Viet Minh spy then she can go to hell, but if not, I don't want her shot out of hand." He said

I looked at him carefully. The worry on his face would have

been amusing in any other circumstances, the happy-go-lucky von Kessler showing concern for a native girl.

"Look, Manfred, the girls will almost certainly be locked away somewhere. If one or both of them is wandering around freely, you know what that means, surely? If they're giving free run of their Headquarters, it could only be because they are trusted members of the Viet Minh."

"Yes, but,"

"No buts," I interrupted him. "If that's the case, they're fair targets for our guns. If they're locked away, they won't get caught in any crossfire."

"I see, yes, I suppose you're right. Dammit, Jurgen, I'm really attached to Thien. We made plans, you know, after the war," he replied.

I was surprised. "Plans? With a native girl? What kind of plans?"

"We wanted to get married. We'd talked about settling down here, perhaps buying a small plantation in the south, near Saigon, after my service was completed."

I looked at him. "Quite the romantic, Corporal? Don't worry, it may never happen. Either way, you'll know soon enough."

He looked downcast. "That's what I'm worried about, Jurgen. Just, be careful, in case it's not her."

"The men have all been briefed, Manfred, so if she's innocent, there's nothing to worry about."

I checked my watch. "About a minute to go, stand by, tell the men to be ready."

He passed the word along, but there really was little need.

They were all tense, waiting for the moment when we hit the enemy HQ. There was a bend in the road about a hundred metres ahead. I saw the Willys disappear around it and heard the distinctive clattering sound of the Browning .30 calibre as it opened fire. Then we were into the bend and almost immediately I could see our objective. It was a Buddhist temple, sure enough, quite a small one but still it seemed sacrilegious to pervert it to the cause of war. The area around the building was occupied by dozens of Viets, most in uniform and carrying a weapon. I cursed our intelligence people. Not only had the cheeky bastards set up an HQ this close to Hanoi, but they were using it openly, perhaps daring the French to do anything about it.

We called their dare. One by one our trucks came into sight of the temple. The heavy machine guns opened fire, spraying thousands of rounds in a matter of less than a minute. Some of the Viets were running for cover. Others, too shocked to respond, just stood open-mouthed as our bullets took them, hurling them to the ground with the sheer weight of lead. The enemy went down as if scythed, by the time we drew up to the temple they were strewn all over the ground, I estimated over a hundred people dead. We dismounted from the vehicles and began deploying.

It was a good plan, decided before we had left the barracks. The machine gunners stayed in their vantage points in the trucks. The rest of us split into groups of twenty, two groups taking the front and back of the temple, two groups checked the outbuildings and surrounding area, while the fifth group, my own with von Kessler, located the statue of Buddha. It stood at the side of the temple, looking solid and heavy, immovable. No wonder our troops had never found it in one of their searches.

Thanks to Trinh, we knew that the appearance was deceptive. Von Kessler went straight to the hidden lever, moved it sideways and two of the men pushed hard on the statue. It tilted over smoothly and lay on the ground on its side leaving an exposed hatchway. I looked in, there were steps leading down. I signalled for the men to follow, then started on down, von Kessler followed behind me.

Almost immediately we heard two voices, speaking in a fairly normal, relaxed tone of voice. It seemed that they were unaware of the attack above ground. Obviously sound did not penetrate this subterranean complex.

Corporal Dubois and Private Laurent, our experts with knives, were behind us. I whispered for them to come forward, then sent them to deal with the owners of the voices. If we could eliminate them silently we would have a good chance of overrunning the underground HQ before they had time to destroy their papers and maps and make a getaway. It was inevitable that they would have more than one escape hatch from this place. The two Arabs slipped forward, there was the sound of a muffled cry, then silence. Dubois came back.

"Both dealt with, Sergeant."

"Well done, Dubois."

I carried on down the stairway and around the corner into the softly lit gloom of the main passage. Laurent was dragging the second of the dead Viets into an opened out space at the side of the tunnel, probably it was used for storage. We were using it for storage too, perhaps of a different kind that its original constructors envisaged. I took the lead again and we pushed on down the tunnel, the rest of the men close behind.

We came across another open doorway in the side of the tunnel. Peering around the gap I could see that it was an armoury, rack upon rack of rifles and submachine guns. I recognised several of the weapons we used, MP40's, Kar 98s, there were Russian made DP28 light machine guns, even, I noticed what looked like a British Vickers Machine gun. Two Viets were busy at a bench. One was filing away at a piece of metal held in a vice, the other was stripping a Kar 98 and wiping it with an oily rag. I nodded at Dubois and Laurent, held up two fingers. Two men to be exterminated. The Arabs edged forward, stepped quietly into the underground chamber, knives drawn. Both had almost reached their targets, slipping forward in a long, fluid movement before the Viets even noticed them. I watched them operate, gracefully swaying forward with their knives held low at their sides, almost as if they were performing a ritual dance. The grace of the movements concealed the speed of their approach, before the enemy even thought to respond they were collapsing with their throats slit from side to side, blood gushing onto the armoury floor.

I sent one of the men with a message to bring Petrov here. There was only one way to deal with this huge amount of ordnance, which was with his unique brand of explosives. Then we moved on. We came to a side room lined with bunk beds, it was a huge space. There must have been as many as thirty double bunk beds in there, all occupied, sixty enemy in all.

Manfred and I covered the further reaches of the tunnel

while the rest of the men went quietly in, their knives and sharpened bayonets drawn. The blades rose and fell. There was the occasional grunt, a muffled cry, a sigh, it was surreal, a shadow dance of death played out in this gloomy cavern concealed beneath the jungles of Indochina. The men filed out, their grisly work done and we moved on. We were nearly at the end of the tunnel, just ahead we could see that it opened out into a room that was brightly lit. We could hear voices, it was a miracle that we had got so far undetected, but now it was time for a direct assault before the rats began to leave their lair. I checked behind me, the men were all ready. I led them forward in a rush and we surged into the main room.

It was a more spacious than we had imagined, about ten metres square. There were three doors opening off it, all closed. I signalled some of the men to go and cover them. Then I returned my attention to the occupants of the room. There were ten of them, Viets, all uniformed except for one, who was clearly the leader. He recovered first from the shock and looked at me with ice in his stare. Some of the others started to grab for weapons, but at a word from him they stopped and held up their hands. Except for one, a young lieutenant, who grabbed for his holstered pistol. Before he could even remove it from the holster, several shots rang out and he fell down, his body split open with the force of the bullets. The sound of the shots was massive in the enclosed space, our ears rang for several minutes afterwards. Then it all went quite again.

I gave orders for the men to secure the prisoners and they were quickly tied with strong twine we carried with this for the purpose. The table in the middle of the room was covered in papers and maps, there was one chair nearby. I ordered one of the men to gather up the papers, then I sat down and pointed at the man in civilian clothes.

"You, what is your name, comrade?"

He walked calmly over to me, his eyes watchful, there was no fear displayed there. Even tied, it was obvious he was searching for any way to turn events to his advantage.

"I am Trinh Ca Tam, Sergeant. I see you are Foreign Legion, from the local barracks in Hanoi, no doubt?"

The bastard was even fishing for information as he answered me. I ignored him.

"You are the commissar of this outfit, I assume, Comrade Trinh?"

He inclined his head gravely.

"I see. Trinh, any relation to Trinh Van Dung?"

He stood silently, but I could see his eyes change slightly at the mention of the name.

"Or should I say the unfortunate Trinh Van Dung?"

That got to him. "You have killed Dung?"

I smiled. "Who are you, his father, uncle, some other relation? No matter. We're looking for two women, Thien and Mai, are you holding them here?"

Again, Trinh gave no answer, but his eyes gave him away as they glanced in the direction of one of the doors.

"Manfred, check that door, be careful. See if the girls are inside, but remember, one of them is a traitor. Get some of the men to check inside the other doors, there may be other enemy troops that we haven't accounted for."

Two men took each of the doorways, one covering the other

as they opened them and leapt though. One was a storeroom, filled with foodstuffs, clothing and ammunition. In the corner there was a simple hand operated printed press, a duplicator. I had seen the leaflets and newspapers that they produced on these primitive devices, they were excellent propaganda tools for the Viet Minh. It would be good to put this one out of use. Another doorway led to a narrow tunnel, the troopers reported back that it led to the surface. Good, that was their escape route uncovered.

Von Kessler rattled on the handle of the last doorway, it was locked.

"The key, Comrade Trinh," I said to the commissar. He ignored me.

"Corporal Dubois, kill the man standing next to the commissar."

Dubois looked at me, surprised, then shrugged his shoulders, drew his knife and walked across to the man standing next to Trinh. A quick slash and the man lay dying on the ground, his blood leaving him as the spark of life departed from his body.

"The key, Comrade Trinh," I said again to the commissar.

"I can keep this up until they're all dead, then we'll start on you."

Silently he glanced down at the left hand pocket of his jacket. I reached in and found the key, then gave it to Manfred. He opened the door cautiously, then with a cry rushed forward. It was a radio room, clearly serving as a holding cell as well.

Thien was lying on the floor, unconscious. Mai was sat next to her on the ground, her hands tied in front of her. Von Kessler rushed in and untied Mai, who painfully got to her feet. He called for a medic, then picked Thien up and carried her into the main room and put her gently on the table, where the medic began checking out her wounds. She was covered in bruises and looked as if she has been systematically tortured for some time.

For several minutes I looked around the room, noting that the radio was fairly modern and powerful with an aerial cable that led out of the room, presumably it was rigged in a tree somewhere up on the surface. Then I drew my pistol. A few minutes later I went back into the main room.

"Does that answer any questions about them?" Manfred asked me angrily.

"Look at the state of them. There's no way they are traitors, they've been badly abused."

"It does look that way," I said to him.

"Jurgen, thank God you got here," Mai said suddenly. She was massaging her arms where they had been bound.

"What happened, Mai?" I asked her.

"They came to a bar where Thien and I were having a drink. We were just sitting there chatting when the Viet Minh, eight of them, burst into the bar and kidnapped us. They brought us here to question us about the Foreign Legion, then they planned to kill us for being collaborators."

"It looks as if Thien has had a bad time of it. Why did they treat her so badly and not you?"

I looked at her eyes, was that evasion I could see in there, or just fear after spending so much time waiting for torture and execution in this Viet Minh dungeon?

She shook her head. "I honestly don't know. I think that I would have been next, I suppose."

"You'd better take it easy for a bit," I said to her, indicating the chair.

"Just sit down while we have a little chat with Comrade Trinh. We're clearing out anything of value while we're waiting for Sergeant Petrov to arrive with his demolition charges, then we can see about getting you home."

She sat down, near to Trinh.

"Thank you, Jurgen, you're very kind."

"Now, Trinh, how many underground bases do you have in the Hanoi area?"

He smiled and said nothing. I showed him my pistol.

"Comrade, I really don't have time for this," I shouted at him. I slashed the barrel of my gun across his face drawing blood.

"I need information, Trinh, how many bases around Hanoi? Do you want me to introduce you to Corporal Dubois? Dubois, show this swine your knife."

The Arab produced his knife and flourished it at the commissar, smiling.

"He'll take your ears off, then your toes, your fingers, he'll cut you into tiny pieces and you'll still be alive to feel it all happening, Trinh. Now talk."

Trinh just stared back at me, silent. I slammed the gun down on the table and grabbed him by the lapels, head butting him in the face. More blood streamed out of his smashed and broken lips, several teeth had fallen out to the floor. I punched him in the face, then the stomach, kneed him in the balls, then gave him several more good uppercuts to the face. He grunted with the pain, almost fell, but two of my men held him on his feet. Von Kessler looked at me quizzically, I didn't normally beat up bound prisoners, wondering what was so important about getting this information out of Trinh now. I hoped it would be worth it.

I slammed my fist into Trinh's stomach again and two more blows to his face. His appearance was ghastly, covered in blood, both eyes closed, his skin beginning to go dark where my blows had landed.

"Talk to me, you bastard," I shouted. "I want a number, how many bases are there?"

Then I felt and arm around my neck and the unmistakable pressure of a gun barrel against the small of my back.

"Stop, Sergeant, leave him alone. You men, get back or I'll kill him."

It was Mai, she had grabbed my pistol from the table and had manoeuvred me around so that I was between her and my men.

"Manfred, untie the commissar, now, or Jurgen will be killed."

He looked desperately at me.

"Don't do it, Manfred. Mai, why are you doing this? Was it all a sham, you and Karl-Heinz Vogelmann?"

She laughed.

"Vogelmann? He was just another French killer, sent here to enslave the Viet people. Sure, I slept with him, but inside he made me sick. 1 was always waiting for the time when we could kill him and all of the French colonialists like him. Manfred, untie Commissar Trinh now, or Jurgen gets it. Hurry!"

"What do I do, Jurgen?" Manfred asked, despair in his voice.

"You do nothing," I told him.

"So Mai, you have always been Viet Minh. What about Thien?"

"Her?" She laughed again.

"A French whore, that's all. Stupid cow. I used to pump her about the Legion's operations on the pretext of concern about Karl-Heinz. She never even realised, but she soon will when she gets what's coming to all collaborators, a bullet in the back of the neck. This is the last time, Manfred. Untie the Commissar or Jurgen dies. Jurgen, order him to untie comrade Trinh, immediately."

"Go fuck yourself, Mai." I replied calmly.

"Very well, Jurgen" she said. "We will all die here together."

She pulled the trigger. There was a loud click. Then another, and another. I turned around and gently took the pistol from her hands, she was too shocked to resist.

"What happened?" she whispered.

"While I was in the radio room I took the bullets out of my gun. I suspected something was badly wrong. Why would the Viets leave two prisoners alone in a room where they could damage a valuable radio transmitter? It was obvious to me that one of you was with the Viets, the only question was, which one? You have helped me immensely, Mai, thank you."

"You bloody Nazi bastard, you, you..." she started beating me with her fists.

"Corporal Dubois," I called, "take her back into the radio room and make sure she never betrays us ever again."

"No, no," she screamed. "Jurgen, please no, don't let him kill me."

I nodded to Dubois. "Make it quick."

He put a meaty hand over her mouth to silence the screams as he dragged her into the radio room. He kicked the door shut and we waited in silence. After less than a minute he came back out and looked at me meaningfully.

"So you're going to kill us all?" Trinh asked me. His eyes blazed with hate, but still no fear was apparent on his bloody and bruised face.

"We're taking you back, Trinh, you and your men. Our intelligence people will be happy to chat with you."

Just then, Petrov arrived.

"You need a big bang, Jurgen?"

"Big as you can make it, Nikolai. Men, start moving these prisoners away, we'll take them back to Hanoi. Watch they don't try any funny business. Two of you carry Thien out, be careful, she's had a hard time. I smiled as Manfred carefully supervised the stretcher party with his girlfriend. We made our way to the surface, leaving Petrov to set his charges.

Outside we met one of our men.

"Did you find Mai as well?" He asked.

I looked at him stone faced. "She's dead."

I told him what happened.

"There was no doubt then, she was working for the enemy?"

"No doubt at all."

"Fucking Viets," he spat out.

He gave me a scathing look and stalked off to help supervise loading the prisoners on the lorries, with the survivors on the surface we had twenty three in all. We were going to be packed in, but our masters in Hanoi would be delighted at the haul. A major Viet Minh base operating under our noses completely destroyed and a bunch of prisoners, including at least one high ranking commissar, to be interrogated.

Their information would be priceless, provided that the right people handled the interrogation. People who would value the lives of thousands of French soldiers higher than their repugnance at having to beat up a few Viet Minh to prise out the information they needed to save the lives of those French soldiers.

"The Captain says we're ready to move out," Sergeant Bauer came to inform me.

"Leforge is deliriously happy with the success of the operation. I think he wants some kind of a triumphal entry into the Hanoi barracks, hail the conquering hero." He grinned.

"I don't think Karl-Heinz would have been impressed, Friedrich. Does Leforge know the full story, about Mai?"

His expression changed. "I see what you mean, I'll go and tell him."

We finished off loading our truck, drove a short distance and stopped. Petrov dismounted and walked back to observe the former Buddhist temple. There was not long to wait before the shattering roar as the underground structure exploded, hurling smoke and flames high into the sky. The temple shook and it literally imploded on itself, falling into the ground and utterly obliterating the Viet Minh tunnel complex.

There was a loud cheer from the men. The distasteful business about Mai aside, it was a great success, a mission to be proud of. An hour later we were sitting in Colonel Joffre's office, where he had opened a bottle of Cognac.

"It's not just good men, it's unbelievable. We've been under a lot of pressure to get results, especially against the local insurgents. This will certainly give them something to think about."

"Do you mean the Viet Minh, Sir, or our High Command?"

Joffre laughed. "Good point, Sergeant Hoffman, truly a good point. I would say both, wouldn't you?"

He raised his glass. "Damnation to the Viet Minh, gentlemen."

"And to the High Command," I added.

We touched glasses. Damnation indeed, to all of them. I had another drink and then made an excuse to leave. I went to the infirmary and found Manfred sat at the side of Thien's bed. She was awake.

"This is progress, Manfred, she looks much better."

Thien looked up at me.

"Thank you, Jurgen, for all you have done. They would have killed me, you know."

"But they didn't, Thien, so you can put that behind you."

I bid them goodnight and went back to my quarters. I stripped off, took a shower and lay on my bed, nursing a bottle of Scotch whisky that I kept for these occasions. I lit a cigarette and lay there smoking, think about all that had happened. Was I wrong to let Giap go?

On reflection I would have done the same thing again. These people were beasts, animals, not fit to inhabit the world of men. To slaughter men indiscriminately, as they did, would reduce me to their level. Certainly I had killed other men, probably hundred of them, directly or indirectly. But there has to be a sound reason, other than pure sadism or following orders, the excuse that our concentration camp guards and Einsatzgruppen gave for murdering countless numbers of Jews and Gypsies. There has to be a moral imperative, otherwise I might just as well put a gun to my head and shoot myself.

I lay there drinking and lighting one cigarette after the other. Then there was a soft knock at the door.

"Enter," I called.

The door opened, it was Helene. I saw a smile on her face, looked down and realised I was still naked.

"Damn, I'll find something to put on, Helene."

"No, I like you just as you are, Jurgen. Stay right there."

She turned the key in the door and came to me. She bent down and kissed me long and passionately. Then she stood up and began to undress.

"You're not too tired, my brave Sergeant?" she asked, amusement in her voice.

"Try me and see, Helene, you can be the judge."

"Certainly Sergeant, I will obey your order."

She laughed out loud and pulled off the last of her underwear. Then she came to me and our bodies melted together.

I felt the tension, the wretchedness of the whole Indochina war, slowly seep out of me as we made slow, sensuous love. Afterwards, we both lit cigarettes.

"Have you thought any more, Helene," I asked her, "about the future for us?"

She looked up at me.

"Not really, my darling. I want us to always be together, but marriage?" She shook her head.

"I will be yours for ever, Jurgen. But I will not marry you while you're fighting this war. Ask me when it's over, or you have left the Legion. For now, let's just enjoy what we have, each and every day."

Two weeks after the mission, I received a long letter. I was sitting in a bar with Friedrich and Nikolai Petrov when a young Viet came in, carrying a package. We were immediately wary and our hands dropped to our guns, but we relaxed when he asked for Sergeant Hoffmann, then handed me the package, which contained a letter, and disappeared out of the door. I looked at the package.

"It's too thin to be a bomb," I remarked.

"For God's sake, Jurgen, open it, it's just a letter," said Nikolai.

I opened the package and read the letter. It was from Vo Nguyen Giap. The letter was simple, a message from one soldier to another. He thanked me for sparing his life. The letter was quite simply to repeat his offer of a job, on his staff.

"I say honestly, Sergeant Hoffmann, that you are one of the most resourceful soldiers I have ever encountered. If you will join me and my struggle for freedom for the peoples of Indochina I can offer you the immediate rank of Senior Colonel, with enhanced pay of $750 per month. You would be able to bring Miss Baptiste with you and we can give you a substantial villa for both of you to live in. In the event that Miss Baptiste accepts your proposal of marriage, you would find a good career and a prosperous and happy life working for the next People's Democratic Republic of Vietnam."

How the hell did the cunning sod know so much about my personal life, I wondered? The letter went on.

"Should you decline my offer, and I do understand the loyalties you have expressed to me, the same sum of money will be placed as a bounty on your head. You are a soldier and you know the rules of the game. I would prefer you to fight on my side, but if not, I will do my utmost to have you killed. Think carefully, Sergeant Hoffmann. You know that the French occupation is doomed. It would be better to avoid being on the losing side for the second time in your life. You will be contacted during the next four weeks for a reply. Giap."

I showed the letter to the others. They laughed. "Better take it to Colonel Joffre, Jurgen, tell him you want a rise or else," Friedrich said.

"Or they'll put a bullet in your head to prevent you joining the enemy," Nikolai warned.

There was a candle burning on our table. I used it to set fire to the letter and burnt it in the ashtray. For a brief moment I thought about it. Colonel Hoffman, aide to Vo Nguyen Giap, second in command to Ho Chi Minh. And the Colonel's lady, Helene. It was some fantasy. I must have been dreaming, because I suddenly heard Friedrich shouting.

"Jurgen, what happened? You went into a trance. Thinking about all that money?"

I shook my head.

"Sorry Friedrich, what did you say?"

"I asked you about Giap's comment, that we would lose the war," he said, puzzlement in his voice.

"Do you remember Russia, the communists, the way they fought, with no regard for human life? The sheer numbers of them, we could kill a thousand and ten thousand would come to take their place. Do you remember all of that?"

"Yes, of course I do," he replied.

"So what's different here, the fight against the Viet Minh?"

He thought for fully a minute. Then he replied.

"Nothing."

Lightning Source UK Ltd.
Milton Keynes UK
UKOW051957220212

187765UK00001B/101/P